HUNTED BY DEMONS

HUNTED BY DEMONS

FIONA ANGWIN

First published in October 2019 by Telos Publishing,
139 Whitstable Road, Canterbury, Kent CT2 8EQ,
United Kingdom

www.telos.co.uk

Telos Publishing values feedback if you have any comments
about this book please email feedback@telos.co.uk

ISBN: 978-1-84583-137-0

British Library Cataloguing in Publication Data. A catalogue
record for this book is available from the British Library.

For my wonderful and supportive husband Richard, who took me to the inspiring city of Rome. For my goddaughter Becky - here is a backstory for you - and for my lovely and supportive readers, who have given me so much encouragement.

I am grateful to Sir Edward Dashwood for giving me permission to 'demonise' The Hellfire Caves.

Finally, I would like to thank Sam, David and Stephen from Telos Publishing for taking a chance on me.

1

Glint crouched behind the model of the 18th century Steward, the figure's frock coat hiding the creature from view. Not that there were many people there to notice him. It was a quiet day in The Hell-Fire Caves, and there weren't a lot of tourists about. Even when the place was busy, people rarely saw him. He'd discovered that humans hardly ever paid attention to anything they weren't expecting to see ... especially nasty little imps.

Glint's talons began to twitch. He was getting bored, waiting for a chance to make some trouble. That's what imps did after all. They were among the Lesser Invisibles, sent into the world to cause chaos whenever rules got broken and humans found out too much about the never-ending battle between the creatures of the Darkness, and the Angels. Although, in Glint's case, he hadn't exactly been sent. He'd just discovered a weak spot between the Darkness and the world. He knew he should probably tell someone about it – some important creature, like a demon – but all the demons ever did was kick him around, so why should he? It was his secret, and he relished the fact that he could sneak into the world whenever he chose, while every other creature in the Darkness had to wait for the rules to be broken before they could come through.

He heard footsteps approaching, and crouched even further back in the small Steward's Cave. He was invisible, of course, but occasionally there were humans who could catch a glimpse of him out of the corner of their eye, or sense his presence, and for Glint, that spoilt his fun. He'd rather remain unseen so that he could play some nasty trick on people, so for now he just kept out of sight, counting on the dummy's period costume, and the desk at which the figure was seated to keep him hidden from anyone who just might be able to see him.

The footsteps belonged to a young couple, a girl with long

dark hair, tied up with a trailing chiffon scarf, dark grey eyes and a turned-up nose. From the bulge around her middle she appeared to be pregnant. The young man was tall and thin, with curly brown hair and hazel eyes, which seemed to twinkle with good humour.

'Not for long,' thought Glint, beginning to creep forward. The imp reached his clawed fingers up onto the desk, where an ancient account book was open, with a few old coins scattered across its surface, and began to move the money around very, very slowly.

'Did you see that?' asked the girl, her hand reaching for the young man's, seeking reassurance. Glint smirked to himself, certain she could only see the inexplicable movement of the coins, and not the grotesque fingers sliding them around. If those were visible, she'd be much more alarmed.

The young man nodded, slowly, unsure what to make of what he was seeing. 'Maybe dis is some kind of moving display, no?' he replied, in a soft Italian accent.

'I don't think so,' said the girl. 'What's the point of making the coins move around like that? If they'd wanted to bring the scene to life, surely they'd animate the model of the steward … have his arm moving or something, so that it looked like he was writing?'

'Whatever is going on, I am not 'appy about it … dey should not do something that might upset you, Phoebe … or de *bambino*.'

'I'm not upset, Marco, just puzzled … and the baby is fine,' replied Phoebe. 'We came here because you like weird, creepy places. You can't complain when it turns out to be just that.'

'Perhaps visiting De Hell-Fire Caves … it was not such a good idea,' Marco answered guiltily.

'Give me the guide book,' said Phoebe, holding out her hand for the slim volume. 'Maybe it says something about it in there.'

'I already looked at it, *caro*,' he said, handing it to her, 'When we were 'aving coffee. It said nothing about anything that moved.'

'Well, we'd better move,' grinned Phoebe. 'There are more

people coming down the tunnel. We don't want to hold them up. And they can hardly squeeze round me … not with the bump.' She placed her hand protectively on her rounded stomach, 'I can't wait to be a normal size again, instead of feeling like an elephant.'

'If you are an elephant, you are a very beautiful one,' Marco replied, 'My favourite elephant in de world.'

Phoebe chuckled, and the couple wandered on, further into the caves, leaving Glint annoyed that he hadn't managed to scare them with his little trick. The imp was about to follow them down the passageway, when a family arrived at the entrance of the Steward's Cave and stopped to look at the display. He decided to stay put and try his little trick on them, to see if he could frighten the children.

Phoebe and Marco walked slowly down through the tunnels, with Phoebe stopping in the better lit sections to read passages out of the guide book. 'These tunnels were dug out with pickaxes in the 18th century, at a time when several harvests had failed and the landowner, Sir Francis Dashwood, was trying to provide employment for the villagers. The chalk that was removed was used to build a road … but the caves that were created … well … Sir Francis had other plans for them.' She grinned at Marco, 'They do like to make it sound creepy, don't they? Oh, there's a bit here about the Steward … I think that's the one we saw the model of earlier … this says he was Paul Whitehead. He was a little-known poet, and his role as Club Steward was to keep a list of the drink consumed by members of the Hell-Fire Club at Medmenham Abbey nearby. Eeeew! Apparently when he died he arranged to have his heart removed and given to Sir Francis. Now that really is creepy.'

'It is de Hell-Fire Club dat interests me,' replied Marco. 'It is said dat dey performed strange rituals down 'ere in the caves … but nobody knows what dey did exactly.'

'Drank at lot, from the sound of it,' Phoebe laughed, 'Come on let's keep going.' As they walked they stopped to look in the smaller caves on either side of the tunnel. These were separated off from the main passageway by barriers, and enlivened with dummies in period costume, depicting elements of the caves' history.

'See,' said Marco, suddenly sprinting ahead, 'models of de ghosts said to be 'aunting de caves.' He pointed to two figures, one wearing a nun's habit, and another in a wedding dress, her hands stained with blood. 'It is said de girl upset de young men in 'er village by falling for a rich gentleman. De local boys tricked 'er into coming out 'ere in 'er bride dress to elope with 'im. When she found just de local boys 'ere she got angry, stones were flung and she was killed. Now she 'aunts de caves ... Sad no?'

'Marco Fanucci, sometimes I worry about you,' said Phoebe as she hurried to catch up. 'You do like the weirdest things.'

'Of course, *caro*, dat is why I like you,' Marco said, laughing.

'You'd better more than like me,' said Phoebe with a grin, 'We're getting married, and I'm carrying your baby.'

'You know 'ow I feel about you,' said Marco, being serious for a moment. "Ere. I 'ave something to show you.' He pulled a bundle of papers out of his inside pocket. 'I 'ave arranged it all ... de 'oneymoon. I will be showing you Rome. A painting trip. As we are both artists it is appropriate, no?'

'That's wonderful, Marco,' chuckled Phoebe, 'but we've only just graduated! I'm not sure we're really artists yet. And the wedding may be next week, but with the baby due in a month who knows when we'll be ready to travel.'

'Dat is why I got dese,' said Marco handing her the papers.

'Open tickets?' Phoebe was amazed. 'How on earth could you afford that?'

'My grandmother in Rome, Nonna Battista, de one who brought me up,' Marco answered. 'Dey are 'er wedding gift to us. So long as we go and visit with 'er when we are over dere. Good, no?'

'Brilliant! That's so kind of her,' said Phoebe. 'I can't wait to thank her. Is she coming to the wedding?'

'Sadly, no,' replied Marco. 'She says she is too old and ill to travel. You'll 'ave to thank her when we go to stay. Now come on, let's explore de caves.'

'I don't know why you're so fascinated by anything macabre,' said Phoebe.

She listened to the sound of occasional droplets of water falling onto the floor of the tunnel, and shivered. The noises seemed to echo like drips splashing into a metal bucket.

'Everything ok, *caro*?' asked Marco.

Phoebe nodded, but she wasn't really sure. She had the strangest feeling that someone was watching them, but in these long tunnels chiselled out of stone there was nowhere for anyone to hide.

Glint observed from behind a pillar as Phoebe and Marco wandered deeper in to the cave system. There was something about them that intrigued him though he could not have explained what it was. Even so, he was determined to follow. Perhaps he'd get the chance to cause some real mischief.

2

Fen was waiting ... he'd spent a lot of time doing that lately. Waiting to forget. Waiting to recover. Waiting to be reassigned. He'd failed – he knew that. As a guardian angel he was supposed to be able to protect people ... and he'd failed. The whole town that was under his protection had been destroyed.

He'd tried to warn everyone of course ... tell them that an earthquake was coming, but who was going to take any notice of an angel that you couldn't even see? Usually angels tried to influence people quietly, whispering positive suggestions into their minds, and hoping that people would listen, and accept what the angel had recommended, while thinking that their course of action was their own idea. That had worked, with a handful of the townsfolk, but he hadn't had time to warn everyone individually. Eventually he'd broken the rules and appeared in the centre of the town, white robes, feathery wings and all. He'd shouted at them to leave before it was too late, but it already was. His appearance had sent some people running into the churches, to pray for protection, not realising that Fen *was* their protection, if they would only listen to him. He felt worst about the ones who were crushed inside the churches when the earthquake hit. He hadn't meant to frighten them, just warn them, but instead he had made things worse by driving them into buildings, when they might have been safer in the streets. And, of course, by breaking the rules like that, he had let a few nasty creatures come through from the Darkness, and the people of the town had had more trouble to deal with.

That had been a while ago: almost twenty years in human terms. Although Fen had lost his sense of time since the earthquake. After that the angel had been sent to protect smaller groups of people, but that assignment hadn't gone well either. He found he just couldn't focus on anything. He slept a lot, when angels don't really need to, and he couldn't bring himself to get attached to any of his charges, which meant he barely even noticed their soul-lights, and what those glowing colours could tell him about the mood and character of their owners. Because of which he didn't realise when things were going wrong for them ... leading to more losses, and subsequent reassignments for Fen.

Now he knew he was an utter failure, as he sat at the graveside of his last charge, or victim, as Fen had come to think of anyone in his care. What was the point of being a guardian angel if you never managed to save anyone, from anything?

'Hello,' said a soft voice close behind him. 'What's your name?'

Fen looked round, horrified. Nobody was meant to be able to see him! But then, he wasn't supposed to be sitting beside a grave, moping. He jumped to his feet, remembering to 'flutter' his wings at the right frequency to make them, and himself, invisible to humans. He couldn't see anyone nearby; the cemetery was deserted. The only figures in view were ancient stone statues of angels, acting as grave markers and memorials.

'Do you miss him very much?' said the voice. 'Your little boy? I miss mine ... he was sweet ... the same age as me, I think. Although I'm not quite sure how old I am!'

Fen jumped as a figure he had assumed to be a stone angel stepped down off a plinth and skipped towards him. She was small, only coming up to his shoulder, and seemed almost childlike, with wavy light blonde hair and bright blue eyes. She was dressed in the traditional long white gown, and her skin was very pale, all adding to the impression he'd had that she was made of marble.

'Well,' she asked again, 'what's your name?'

'I'm called Fen' he said. 'It's short for Defender.' He wondered why he'd even bothered to add that information, when he was so obviously bad at defending anyone.

'I'm called Saraf,' said the little angel, staring at him. 'Why is your hair grey? Is it because it matches your eyes?'

Fen didn't want to get into that conversation - his eyes, of course, had always been grey - but his hair had turned that colour slowly, after the earthquake, as he had struggled to come to terms with losing so many of the people he'd been responsible for.

Not waiting for him to answer, she laid the bundle of flowers she was holding on the grave that Fen had been sitting beside. 'There, that will make him feel better, won't it?'

'I'm not sure it will,' answered Fen. 'Given that he's dead. I suspect that he's not feeling anything anymore.'

'Then he's not in pain anymore either, which is good, isn't it?' Saraf replied cheerfully.

'No,' snapped Fen, 'Because he wasn't in pain before ... he was just upset. His girlfriend dumped him, and he got very drunk and walked in front of a car.'

'Oh, you poor angel! A suicide! They're the worst. You must be feeling terrible that you couldn't reach out to him, influence him and change his mind. But you mustn't blame yourself. It's not your fault ... I'm sure you tried your best.' Saraf smiled at Fen in an attempt to comfort him.

Fen cringed inside. He hadn't tried, he hadn't even noticed how upset and drunk his charge was. The young man hadn't committed suicide, his death was just a stupid accident, as the boy had staggered into the road without looking. If Fen had been paying attention, he might have been able to stop the boy getting into that state, or prevented the car from colliding with him, or pulled the young man back onto the pavemen.t There were lots of ways he could have saved him. He just ... didn't.

'What was special about him?' asked Saraf, undeterred by Fen's silence. 'Why did he have a guardian angel anyway? Not everyone has their own, do they? Sometimes there's just one angel to guard a whole city.' Fen shrugged, realising that he'd never thought to ask why he'd been sent to watch over that particular human. More guilt. He turned away, determined to head for the exit of the cemetery. He had no reason to be there anyway, it was just that, with the young man he was supposed to protect dead, he didn't have anywhere else to be either.

'Aren't you going to ask about mine?' the young angel

persisted. 'I asked you about the one you lost ... you ought to ask me about mine. I'm grieving too.'

Fen groaned and turned back to face Saraf. 'All right,' he growled, reluctantly, 'Tell me about yours.'

'He was lovely,' said Saraf, smiling broadly. 'A really sweet boy ... about fifteen years old, and clever. He was very, very clever. He could make things out of metal and invent machines too ... and then he died. It was the plague and I couldn't do anything about it.'

'The plague?' Fen was astonished, 'When was this? What year, I mean?'

'A long time ago,' Saraf replied. 'In the 1300s I think.'

'But it's ... 1999 now,' said Fen, shocked. 'Surely you've protected other people since then?'

'I don't know,' answered Saraf, 'I can't remember.'

Fen looked at her, puzzled. He'd met other guardian angels over the years, but none of them had seemed so childlike. Why would they, when they were all of an age? All alive from the beginning of human history, and entrusted by *Him* to protect the humans *He* seemed to care about so much. So why did Saraf seem so much younger, and why couldn't she remember what she'd done and who she'd protected for the last several hundred years? It didn't make sense.

Still, none of it was his problem. He wasn't responsible for other angels, just for whichever human he was told to protect next. Not that he'd been assigned anyone yet, which was a good thing as far as he was concerned, given how poor his track record had been over the last twenty years. He turned away for a second time, heading for the gate of the cemetery, determined to wash his hands of this strange, lost angelic creature. She wasn't his problem, after all, which was just as well.

'Don't leave me,' she called out, sounding a little panicky. 'I get frightened all on my own.'

'But we usually are on our own,' replied Fen, 'Apart from the humans we look after, and they don't really count.'

'Don't they?' queried Saraf. 'I'm not sure *He'd* agree with you. *He* thinks they're really important, doesn't *He*?'

'I suppose so,' agreed Fen. 'But that doesn't make them good company. Spending years trying to protect someone who can't see you, hear you or talk to you isn't exactly my idea of fun. No wonder we lose interest in our charges.'

'No, we don't,' protested Saraf. 'We're not supposed to, anyway. You're bound to be given someone new to look after soon, and maybe next time you'll be assigned somebody you find interesting.'

Fen doubted it. It was a long time since he'd been curious about anyone he was supposed to be protecting. They all seemed much the same to him. However, he didn't see the point in arguing with this fearlessly positive angel. He had a feeling that none of his negative comments would get through to her.

'You'll find out soon enough, anyway,' continued Saraf. 'I've been sent to fetch you. Come on. Let's go and find out who you're looking after next.'

Fen groaned. Not only did he have another unwanted assignment, but he was stuck with a boundlessly enthusiastic angel for company on the way.

3

Phoebe and Marco had nearly reached the back of the cave system when they came to the illuminated area marked as the River Styx.

'Now this *is* lovely,' said Phoebe, staring at the colourfully lit stalagmites and stalactites reflected in the shallow water. 'I wouldn't mind painting an image like that.' She got out her camera and took a photograph as a reminder, but Marco was already hurrying on.

'Look, Phoebe. 'Ere we are. De Inner Temple.' Marco gestured to the final cave, dressed with dummies in 18th century costume. 'Dis is where dey performed de rituals, according to de legends.'

Since her camera was still in her hand, Phoebe took a picture of Marco, smiling at her as he stood in front of the illuminated cavern, then she moved forward to stand beside him, their hands touching as they both leaned against the wooden rail which acted as a barrier to keep people out of the final cave area.

'What rituals?' she asked. 'And why are you so interested in this stuff?'

'It is fascinating, is it not? De appeal of de darkness. Of all dat is sinister and surreal? Dis book is not clear what rituals were performed but it might be dat people attempted to summon de Devil 'imself.' Marco grinned at Phoebe. 'Exciting, no?'

'No,' said Phoebe firmly, 'You know I don't believe in any of that stuff, not in devils or superstitions … Not even in church stuff.'

'Church stuff?' Marco laughed. 'Oh, Phoebe, you shall 'ave to do better dan dat when you meet my grandmother. She is a great believer, and she brought me up to have faith also.'

'I can respect that, Marco,' replied Phoebe. 'Just don't expect me to believe it. I was brought up to be a bit more sceptical. Anyway, your faith is more about churches and cathedrals, isn't it? So what's with your fascination with all this stuff … rituals and ghosts and evil?'

'It is just de other side of de same coin,' he shrugged. 'Don't look so serious, *caro*. I do not wish to be evil, only to understand it … paint it. Expose it to de world! It stirs my … *immaginazione*. My imagination. Come, you 'ave walked enough. Let us go back.'

'Yes,' agreed Phoebe, 'I fancy a cup of tea before we drive home, if the café is still open.' She turned away from the display in the Inner Temple, but as she took her hand off the wooden rail, she caught her palm on a sizable splinter. 'Ouch,' she muttered, inspecting her hand, which now had a long cut across it. 'That hurts.'

'Let me see,' said Marco, taking her by the wrist. 'You are bleeding! 'Ere, take my 'andkerchief.'

Phoebe grinned. Marco was the only man she knew who ever had a proper hanky. What's more, his hankies were always clean and pressed and ready to use. She suspected that his grandmother had brought him up to always carry them precisely to be able to offer them to maidens in distress - not that she was in distress, or technically a maiden either, since she was several months pregnant.

She looked down at her hand again. The blood was pooling in her palm, and as she reached out to take the handkerchief a few drops of it dripped onto the stone floor. She tried to bind the cut herself, but Marco quickly took over, since tying a knot with one hand was obviously difficult.

'Dere,' he said, smiling at her. 'Dat should stop it bleeding. Now let's go and get you a cup of tea … de English cure for all ills.'

'So long as you're sure you've had enough of all this macabre stuff,' she said with a grin.

'Enough for today, anyway,' Marco chuckled. 'Though I 'ave some interesting locations planned for our trip to Rome … so many places I want to show you … So many wonderful things planned for us to paint.' Phoebe reached up and kissed him and the baby kicked inside her just as their lips touched. The two of them burst out laughing and wandered back up the tunnel hand in hand.

Glint waited until they were out of sight and then slipped out from behind a stalagmite and scampered over to the spot where they'd been standing. His clawed feet happened to touch one of the drops of blood on the ground and he felt a strange sensation. ... So strange that he dropped down onto his scaly stomach to inspect the blood more closely. The smaller spots were drying already but there were still three drops glistening redly on the floor. The imp stretched out his long, pointed tongue and lapped up the blood ... Something was wrong! Glint contorted on the rough surface. It felt as if his whole body was burning. He could hear footsteps approaching and twisted and crawled his way back to the water nearby, slithering into it just as more visitors appeared around the bend. Even soaking in the cool water didn't seem to stop his body feeling hot and painful. Something was very wrong ... and the only thing that could have caused it was the girl's blood. He couldn't remember if he'd ever tasted human blood before, but decided that he couldn't have: he was sure he would have remembered if his body had reacted like that!

When the next group of visitors to the caves had gone, Glint hauled himself out of the water. He felt he needed to follow the girl and see if she was still bleeding, but before he could scramble back onto the path he slipped on the wet rocks. Reaching out a claw to steady himself he glanced down into the water, saw his own reflection, and nearly slipped again. He had changed! His body was slightly bigger, smoother ... a little more demon-like. If that was what just a few drops of human blood could do ... he wanted more. He began to scuttle along the tunnels towards the surface, hoping he could catch up with the couple before they left.

By the time Glint reached the entrance to the cave system the two young people were leaving the café and walking towards the main gate. The girl's hand was no longer bound in the white cloth, which made him briefly hope that he might be able to get one or two more drops of blood, but the wound must have stopped bleeding. It appeared he was out of luck.

Marco had parked his battered yellow 2CV car in one of the handful of parking spaces in front of the entrance to The Hell-Fire Caves, and hurried forward to unlock the front passenger door and hold it open for Phoebe.

'Dere,' he said. 'Aren't you glad dat I insisted in parking up 'ere instead of you having to walk down the 'ill to the big car park, yes?'

'I don't mind walking, Marco ... I'm not ill, I'm pregnant,' protested Phoebe, as she got into the car.

'And I'm just trying to look after you ... and de *bambino*,' he replied with a grin. 'Come on, let's go 'ome.' He opened the back door of the car to drop his coat onto the seat. He was just about to close it when Phoebe said, 'Wait a minute, now we're outside again, I'm too hot.' She scrambled out of the car to take off her own coat, and Marco gallantly turned to help her shrug herself out of it.

Seeing the rear door open and unwatched, Glint made a spur of the moment decision and climbed into the car, tucking himself into the space below the old-fashioned bolted-in seats. By the time Marco threw Phoebe's coat onto the back seat the imp was out of sight, even if Marco had been able to see him.

Marco shut the rear door, then closed Phoebe's door for her, to save her having to reach for it, before walking around the car to get into the driver's seat.

Phoebe couldn't help grinning. After more than two years together he was just as charming and courteous as he'd been on their first date. She still couldn't decide if it was his soft Italian accent or his old-fashioned manners that had attracted her the most when she'd first noticed him. They met at Art School in Bristol, where they were taking many of the same classes, although it had taken them months to start dating ... they'd become such good friends so quickly that neither of them wanted to risk their friendship by becoming a couple.

Now they were only a week away from their wedding, looking forward to spending a lifetime together. Just them, their baby, and their art.

'Soon we will 'ave our little baby. It will have so many opportunities being born into a new millennium'

'Don't call our baby *it!*' objected Phoebe, 'And the new millennium doesn't start for another six months, so there's no need get too excited about it. I certainly don't want to stay pregnant that long, just so our child is born at the turn of the century. Besides, I think babies come out when they're ready. They don't hang around waiting for special dates on a calendar.' Phoebe stretched back in her seat.

''appy?' asked Marco as he backed the car out of the parking space and turned it round.

'Very,' answered Phoebe, grinning at him. 'And I can't believe we're going to Rome for our honeymoon.'

'I very much want you to meet my *nonna* ... grandmother. And dere is so much to paint, not just in Rome. I 'ope to take you to some of my favourite places around Napoli also' he said, smiling at her.

'Any chance you'll paint anything bright and cheerful, or are you still determined to create gloom and despair?'

'Gloom and despair of course,' he chuckled. 'In 'onour of you. It is only because you make me so 'appy dat I can paint de grimmer side of life, paint death itself. Without you, it would draw me in and make me sad.'

'Great,' laughed Phoebe, as the car joined the main road that would lead them back to Bristol. 'I make you so happy that you can afford to be miserable.'

'I am never miserable when I'm with you, *caro*. Now, 'ow many wedding tasks must we do when we get 'ome? I know you, my love. I am sure you will 'ave a list.' He flicked the radio on and they both laughed as Ricky Martin's voice rang out singing 'Livin La Vida Loca.'

'That'll be us,' chuckled Phoebe as they sang along, 'Living the Crazy Life.' She couldn't wait.

As the young couple chatted about their upcoming wedding,

Glint crept out from under the rear seat. He was panicking a little. He'd never travelled so far away from The Hell-Fire Caves before and had no idea how he would return there. It occurred to him that it was the only place he knew of where he could get back into the Darkness.

He was trapped.

4

Fen walked out of the High Council chamber feeling stunned. Part of his brain noticed that stunned felt slightly different to numb, which was how he'd felt for the last twenty or so years, but he wasn't sure it was an improvement. He was still struggling to come to terms with what he'd just been told when Saraf came skipping towards him, smiling and excited.

'Well,' she asked, 'Did they give you someone new to protect? Who? And Why? Are you excited? I'd be excited. I do hope they give me a new assignment soon. It's boring not having anyone to protect.'

Fen tried to focus his attention on Saraf, but his head was still spinning with the information he'd just been given about his new charge.

'She has angel blood,' he muttered in wonder, partly to Saraf, and partly to himself, trying to get his head around the very idea.

'Who does?' asked Saraf in wonder, 'Your new charge? The one you're going to protect? You must be thrilled! I know that we can't protect all the humans individually, there are so many of them, and so few angels. That's why we all start out protecting such large groups, whole populations of cities or towns. And if that goes wrong …' Fen flinched, and Saraf stopped in the middle of her sentence, looking guilty. 'Sorry Fen. I didn't mean to remind you.'

'You didn't,' Fen growled, 'I've never forgotten. A whole town, which I'd protected for generations. Where I knew the names of everyone who lived there. Their stories. Their joys and their sorrows. I'd protected them from so many dangers. Sometimes from situations the people never even knew about, because I'd prevented the trouble from surfacing in the first place but I couldn't save them from the earthquake. I let them down.'

Saraf slipped her hand into his and continued 'And when that happens, and an angel can't cope with the pressure, or the feelings of failure, they get sent to protect smaller groups, more manageable situations, or even just one person who needs to be specially protected by a guardian angel of their own for some reason.'

'For all the good it does,' said Fen, mournfully. 'Whatever I do, everyone dies.'

'Of course they do eventually,' said Saraf, smiling. 'We can't stop that, but we can try to keep them safe up to that point. Prevent the pointless accidents, protect them from evil. Did I tell you about my boy? He died from the plague, but he was so clever. He was an inventor. Some of the things he invented helped people who were ill. That was why he had his own guardian angel, because he was so brilliant. He could have gone on to do so much more if I could have saved him,' Saraf went quiet for a moment, her eyes filling with tears. She pulled her hand out of Fen's to rub the tears away with the back of it and asked, 'What was special about that boy of yours, the one who got run over? You never said.'

'I don't know,' said Fen, with a shrug. 'I never asked. What does it matter anyway? He's dead now.'

'And now the High Council have given you somebody new to look after. Lucky you,' said Saraf.

'I don't feel lucky,' answered Fen. 'I feel completely out of my depth. She has angel blood, apparently. That's why she needs her own guardian angel . Though she's already a young woman, so she must have managed fine without one up to now.'

'Angel blood?' said Saraf, her eyes shining with wonder. 'You mean like in the old story? The Legend of Eskarron? The angel who fell in love with a human?'

'According to the High Council, it's not just a story. Apparently, the angel Eskarron really did fall in love with a human, a woman called Phyllida. Because he loved her so much, he begged to be allowed to put aside his angel status, and live on earth as a human. Remarkably, *He* took pity on Eskarron and granted the angel's request. Having created love, *He* could hardly punish an angel for falling in love so intensely.'

'And your new charge has angel blood? How exciting!' said Saraf, practically bouncing up and down in front of him.

'She's one of Eskarron's descendants. Although Eskarron put aside his powers and his role as an angel, when he married Phyllida he was still of angel stock, and their children had angel blood in their veins. Even though it's been diluted down the generations, his descendants are still connected to all of us. They still have angel blood running through their bodies.'

Saraf turned away from him, her shoulders slumped in sorrow. Fen felt like walking away, getting on with his own duties, now he'd been assigned them, but Saraf seemed so unhappy he didn't feel he could just turn his back on her. He moved closer to the miserable little angel.

'What's wrong?' he asked. 'Why are you so sad?' He realised with surprise that it was the first time he'd paid attention to someone else's feelings for over twenty years.

'I'm not sad,' Saraf snuffled. 'Not for you. I'm glad the High Council have given you someone new to protect ... someone so special. I just wish they'd assign someone to me. I've been waiting for hundreds of years. I must be so bad at doing my job.'

Fen stared at her back feeling helpless. His fellow angel looked so dispirited. Even her white, feathery wings seemed to droop, but he wasn't sure how to help her, or even why he wanted to.

'I'm sure you're very good at the job,' he said in an awkward attempt to cheer Saraf up. 'Better than me, anyway. At least you care more than I do these days. They're bound to give you someone to protect, sooner or later.'

'But I've been waiting for so long!' she spun round to face him, exasperated. 'If they don't give me someone to protect soon, I'll go mad.' Fen wondered if perhaps she already had, but he bit back the comment, not wanting to hurt her feelings. She stared into his eyes for a moment, then suddenly her face lit up.

'I'll come with you!' Saraf declared. 'I'll help you to look after your new person. If both of us think we can't do the job well enough on our own, perhaps we can work together. It'll be perfect.'

Fen wanted to say just how unperfect he thought the idea was, to say nothing of not being authorised by the High Council. He wanted to turn and walk away, but he knew that if he did, Saraf would be crushed, and he simply didn't have the heart to do that to her.

'All right then,' Fen groaned, 'Just for a while, the first day or two, maybe while I figure out why she suddenly needs protecting.'

Saraf flung her arms around him and he pulled back, horrified.

'Just one condition' Fen stated, 'No hugging. Definitely no hugging. And I'm in charge.'

'Of course, Fen' agreed Saraf, smiling broadly. 'I'll be good. I'll do exactly what you tell me.'

Somehow Fen had his doubts about that.

5

Glint had been regretting his decision for the past few minutes. Creeping into the bone shaking old car had been a big mistake. Just because he'd wanted a few more drops of human blood, he was now being carried further and further away from home. Not that the Darkness was exactly homelike, but it was all he knew. He wanted to get back to the other imps, to show off the changes a few drops of blood had made to his ugly body but now he might never return there again.

He peered out from beneath the seat, wondering what to do next, if there was any way to get these humans to turn the vehicle around and take him home. He'd never been in a car before, but he'd seen people driving them. It seemed to be all about how they moved their hands, and turned the wheel. The imp wriggled forward, sliding into the gap under the driver's seat, and reached up his long, clawed fingers to grab the steering wheel.

Marco couldn't see Glint's fingers, but he could feel something tugging at the wheel. He braced his back against the seat and grappled with the car, trying to force it back under control, but although the imp was small, he was very strong, and the wheel kept twisting one way and then the other. What Glint couldn't see from beneath the seat was that the car was travelling along a dual carriageway, surrounded by other vehicles, which in turn were trying to dodge the little 2CV as it jerked about on the road.

'Marco,' shrieked Phoebe, 'What's happening?'

'Dere's something wrong,' replied Marco, trying to manoeuvre the car towards the inside lane, hoping to pull it off the road. 'De steering ... it is not working. 'Old on tight, *caro*.'

Glint gave another hard tug on the steering wheel and the car spun round in a circle, crashed into the side of an estate car, and almost toppled over. Glint let go of the wheel and shrank back under the seat, terrified, just as Marco got the car back under control. Too late. A wagon came up behind them, braked, but couldn't stop in time. It ploughed into the back of Marco's little car, shunting it off the road onto the hard shoulder with such speed that it overshot the safety area, slipped down a steep bank and began to roll over and over, tossing Phoebe and Marco around, only held in place by their seatbelts. Their screams of terror masked those Glint was letting out as he too was thrown about in the car, and felt one of his arms crack as it became entangled with Marco's legs.

Eventually the 2CV came to rest, the right way up, as they had always been designed to do, and there was silence. From the road above people were shouting as some other cars shunted into each other, and a few pulled over to check on the little yellow car they had seen roll down the bank. Looking down at the scrunched wreckage they could see the driver's arm flung out of the window. It wasn't moving.

In the silence Glint watched pools of blood forming beneath the driver's seat. Twisting his own damaged body round he reached forward to lick up a few drops, but somehow it didn't taste quite the same as the girl's had earlier, nor did it have the same effect on him. The imp snarled in frustration. He'd gone to all that trouble and hadn't gained anything from it, except a long walk back to The Hell-Fire Caves.

It dawned on him that he might be in trouble too. Imps didn't have the authority to harm humans – that was the prerogative of the demons. Still, surely, he wouldn't be punished for doing so by accident, would he? Anyway, it wasn't as if any of the demons knew that he was in the human world. Usually Lesser Invisibles like him only came though when the rules got broken. But since he'd found his secret route between the worlds he'd been coming and going as he chose. And if nobody knew he was there, he couldn't be blamed for what happened, could he?

The imp opened the rear door on the passenger side and crawled out, noticing that the door next to the girl had sprung open. There was a trickle of blood running down her wrist, and he couldn't resist lapping at it, but as soon as he swallowed the first few drops shockwaves ran through his body and he had to pull away. People were scrambling down the bank towards the car, so he crawled under it, out of sight, to hide until they were gone.

Fen and Saraf looked down on the battered car, as the ambulance crew pulled Phoebe and Marco out and gently laid them on stretchers before carrying them up the bank and into the waiting ambulances.

Fen couldn't believe what he was seeing. He'd only just been assigned to be Phoebe's guardian and there she was, being put into an ambulance.

'I'm so sorry,' said Saraf. 'You must feel terrible, but at least, if it's something normal, like a car accident, there probably wouldn't have been anything you could have done to stop it happening, or to help her.'

Fen knew that what she said was true, but it didn't make him feel any better. It just gave him another reason not to get attached to his human charges.

'Is she still alive? Can you see her soul-light?' asked Saraf. Fen nodded, slowly. Now he'd been appointed as her Guardian Phoebe's soul-light was the only one he could see. Generally, angels could only see the soul-lights of anyone and everyone who was their responsibly.

'It's very faint … fluttery … I'm not sure if she's going to survive.'

Saraf slipped her hand into his trying to give comfort. 'She might … you don't know yet. What colour is it? I love all the different colours. They tell you so much about a person. What they're like, how they're feeling.'

Fen looked at the girl's soul-light, flickering weakly, and tinged with the icy blue of fear. What colour it would be normally he had no idea and he thought it was unlikely that he would ever find out.

'Soul-lights are so pretty,' continued Saraf. 'All soft and fuzzy. Like fairy-lights. My favourite one belonged to my boy. His was beautiful.'

She turned to look at Fen. He obviously wasn't listening to her. He was staring after the ambulances as they drove away, wondering if it was even worth following them, or if the girl would be dead before she reached the hospital.

Saraf thought she saw something moving out of the corner of her eye, under the smashed up yellow car. Something dark. Something bad. She looked at it more closely, then swung round, reaching out to tug at Fen's sleeve, to get his attention, but the angel was already in the air, preparing to follow the emergency vehicles to the hospital.

'Fen,' she called, 'It wasn't an accident. There's an imp—'

But her fellow angel was gone. Saraf was torn. Should she follow Fen, support him? Help him to try and save the girl? Or should she find out what the imp was up to?

6

Fen landed on the roof of the hospital. Silent and invisible, he made his way down to the accident and emergency department. He'd been in enough hospitals to know that these were always on the ground floor, so that patients could be delivered to the department as quickly as possible.

The ambulances had already unloaded their trolleys and wheeled them into the department by the time Fen got there. Phoebe was agitated ... drifting in and out of consciousness and calling out 'Marco' in her more lucid moments. Fen was just relieved to see that she was still alive. He'd begun to think that he'd lost his charge almost as soon as she'd been assigned to him. The young man on the other trolley was a different matter: he was lying very still. It was worrying. Fen assumed that this was who Phoebe was calling for when he noticed the engagement ring on the girl's finger as her hand clutched at the blanket covering her. It didn't look to the angel as if she was likely to get a reassuring answer.

Fen couldn't detect any un-natural aspects to the condition of either of the young people. Nothing he needed to try and warn the doctors about, so there was no reason for him to have to get directly involved in their treatment. All he could do was wait – just like any concerned friend or relative. Although there wouldn't be anyone coming to find him to give him any news: good or bad. He felt he should be more alarmed, but he hadn't even met Phoebe properly yet, and her fiancé wasn't his problem at all, so all he could do was hang around feeling slightly guilty. It looked as if this assignment was going to turn out just like all the rest. Hopeless and depressing. He began to wonder why the High Council had chosen such a useless guardian for the girl, if she was so important and she really had angel blood. Surely there were other, better angels who could have been given the job? Although Fen knew that there weren't enough angels to look after everybody ... but in that case, why hadn't Saraf been given anyone to protect in hundreds of years? She probably wouldn't be the best Guardian angel, given how childlike she seemed, but at least she'd care about whoever she was looking after. Probably too much.

Fen leaned against a pillar, watching all the activity in the A&E department, letting it flow around him. Then it dawned on him: Saraf wasn't there. He hadn't seen her since they were together at the roadside, looking down at the crashed car. No wonder it was so quiet.

Of course, in human terms it wasn't silent at all, he was surrounded by the noise and bustle of doctors, nurses and patients, all hurrying about their business, but nobody was talking to him, specifically, trying to get his attention by going on about their dead boy. Fen smiled, enjoying the relative peace and quiet for a moment. Then suddenly, he found himself worrying, which was odd really. It wasn't as if Saraf was his responsibility. In fact she didn't seem to be anybody's. She just drifted about like a lost soul with nobody to protect, or to protect her. Fen glanced around the department again. The doctors were working on Phoebe and Marco. Phoebe seemed to have passed out, so if there was nothing he could do to help, he might as well go and see what kind of trouble Saraf had got herself into.

Saraf had crept along behind Glint. The Lesser Invisible puzzled her ... He was big for an imp, and unusual looking. Like something between an imp and a demon. He'd also started off holding his arm awkwardly, when he'd pulled himself out from under the crashed car, trying not to put any strain on it, but as he walked along ducking in and out of the ditch beside the main road, he seemed to move it more easily, as if it no longer caused him any pain, which seemed decidedly strange. They tramped along for quite a long time, with Glint hiding from any passing humans, and Saraf hiding from Glint.

Eventually they left the main roads and made their way up some country lanes until they reached a pair of large iron gates, the entrance to the courtyard of The Hell-Fire Caves.

The angel found the name rather alarming, but having followed the imp this far, she felt she should continue. That way she'd have something useful to tell Fen when she caught up with him.

Glint tucked himself behind one of the litter bins in the courtyard as the final visitors of the day made their way out, and the staff locked up and closed the great iron gates behind them as they set off for home. Saraf had hidden herself behind one of the columns of what appeared to be a church tower, built over the cave entrance, but in fact was just a façade, which troubled her. Who would build just the front of a church tower and not the rest of it?

At the bottom of the tower were smaller iron gates which had also been locked, but as she watched Saraf saw the imp come out of hiding and scurry towards them, squeezing between the bars. She heard his footsteps pattering down the passageway into the cave system.

Saraf flew gently down to the ground and approached the gates. They were locked, and she was too big to squeeze between the bars, but when she touched the keyhole she heard the mechanism click, and the gates swung open. She smiled, strolled down the corridor into the caves, and began to search for the imp.

Saraf wasn't the only creature looking for Glint. Not that the imp knew that anyone was interested in him. He practically bounced along through the caverns, rushing to get to the area called the River Styx. When he reached the spot, he vaulted over the wooden barrier and landed on a large rock sticking out of the water, then glanced down to study his reflection. The few extra drops of blood he'd licked up from the girl's arm had been worth it. He was bigger, stronger - more handsome. Well, in demon terms, anyway. He wasn't a full sized, full strength demon by any means, but those drops of blood had definitely empowered him. What's more, his broken bones had mended themselves: he felt invincible.

As he admired himself, Glint decided that his new body deserved a new name ... something darker, more menacing. Not that he could think of anything yet, but he'd come up with something eventually and make the other imps call him that too! It would be easy enough. After all, he was now more powerful than any of them.

He gazed at his refection in the water and chuckled to himself. It was the last time a smile was going to cross his face for a very long time. His smug self-congratulation was cut off in mid-flow, as something much larger and nastier than he was grabbed him by the back of the neck and flung him against the nearest stalactite. After smashing into it, Glint tried to cling on, but a well-placed foot kicked him loose, and he ended up dropping into the water. He scrambled out and turned to face the creature that had just attacked him. He gulped.

The demon's name was Dread, and he was the nearest thing the imp had to a master. Imps and other Lesser Invisibles were not expected to serve only one demon in the Darkness: they were supposed to follow orders, whichever demon gave them, but often an imp would find one particular demon bossed them around more than the others. Concepts like loyalty and friendship did not exist there but familiarity sometimes built a kind of bond, usually based on an expectation of instant obedience. The better an imp got to know a demon, the more this the demon could come up with vicious ways to torture him.

'I came looking for you, you worm,' boomed Dread. 'You should be honoured. I had a task for you, and you weren't there. So I tracked you down. At first I thought my imp couldn't have just disappeared. There's nowhere to hide in the Darkness. Nowhere that I can't find you. So I searched. I went looking where the other imps said you often hung about and what did I find? A way through. A weak spot.

Somewhere I could get into this world without being invited. But then I thought that can't be right. Because if my loyal imp Glint had discovered such a thing, HE WOULD HAVE TOLD ME!'

Dread's fist smashed into Glint, who squealed. Saraf, hidden behind a pillar of stone, jumped in shock. She hated bullies and was tempted to leap out and defend the smaller creature, even if it was an imp, but something held her back. She needed to know how much trouble the world was in, because if the creatures of the Darkness could come into this world whenever it suited them - without an invitation - without the rules being broken - then she and Fen would have far more to worry about than simply defending one girl. Whichever type of blood ran through her veins.

7

Fen had flown back to the scene of the accident. The car was still there, but there was no sign of Saraf. He looked around, trying to find some clue as to where the young angel could have gone. He saw a trail of flattened plants that seemed to lead from the car towards the ditch that ran beside the road. Why would Saraf walk along a ditch when she could simply fly? There was only one way to find out. Fen lifted himself into the air and flew above the ditch, following the trail; making sure to keep himself invisible. The only problem was that he was flying away from the hospital - where the girl he was supposed to be protecting might have need of him - and towards goodness knew what, to protect an angel for whom he had no responsibility at all. He just hoped he was making the right decision, but he felt it had to be: worrying about Saraf was the first time he'd felt anything other than guilt for years.

He followed the ditch for some distance, then changed direction when he reached the point where the plants in it were no longer crushed, and began to fly over the surrounding area, searching for any signs that might show him which way she had gone next.

Dread was holding Glint up in the air, the demon's claws digging into the back of the imp's scaly neck, as the Lesser Invisible twisted and turned helplessly, straining to escape. The demon leaned in, face to face with Glint, and licked his lips.

'You know I'm going to be punishing you for this, don't you? I'll make you suffer unspeakable torments for a very, very long time. But first, you're going to tell me a few things, like what's happened to you since I last saw you because you didn't look like THIS then.' Dread flung the smaller creature against the rocks, splitting the skin on Glint's face open, and the dark, sludgy liquid that flowed through the imp's veins began to leak out. Dread sniffed the air, intrigued.

'You smell different,' continued the demon, his voice sounding calm and reasonable for a moment, 'And you look different. There must be a reason. Tell me what it is?'

Glint shook his head, helplessly. How could he explain that he'd drunk some drops of a girl's blood, followed her, caused an accident that had injured her, and then licked up some more blood from that. He'd get into terrible trouble. Dread leaned over him, his jaws twitching, preparing to bite the imp's head off and Glint had to face the fact the he was already in trouble … the kind of trouble that was about to be fatal.

'All right, all right,' whimpered the imp. 'I'll tell you.'

Saraf listened, horrified, to what the imp had to say. So, she had been right, the car crash wasn't an accident at all and Phoebe's blood was powerful. No wonder the girl needed a guardian angel. Especially now some creatures from the Darkness knew about her. The angel peered around the stone pillar and watched in horror as the demon licked his misshapen lips.

Saraf could hardly bear to look at the demon. The knowledge that he had once been an angel, like her, but had chosen to rebel, to abandon any loyalty to *Him*, who had created them, horrified her. This was what a fallen angel looked like? It was worse than she had ever imagined. Their lumpen, hideous bodies were not some kind of divine punishment. No. They were just the effects of thousands of years of rage and hatred, twisting them so much in their spirits that the emotions began to colour their shape and their appearance. She found the smell almost unbearable too; a scent of death and decay like rotting flesh. It reminded her of the stink of the plague pits. She shook her head, trying to shake off the memories of her dead boy, and concentrate on what the demon was saying.

'So, if drinking some of the girl's blood made you bigger and stronger and more powerful, drinking yours might do the same for me,' mused Dread. 'Let's find out shall we?' Glint gave a wail that was filled with so much terror that Saraf couldn't bear it any longer. Whatever the imp had done, no creature deserved to be eaten by a bloodthirsty demon intent on causing as much pain as possible.

The angel leapt forward, grabbing Dread by the shoulders and trying to tear him away from the imp. She discovered then that he was much stronger than she'd expected him to be and she realised to her horror that she couldn't remember what to do next ... how to fight a demon. Saraf couldn't remember very much at all. Apart from about the boy she'd protected, all those years ago. She realised she'd made a major mistake, charging into battle without any kind of plan, but she couldn't help herself. Usually a demon couldn't come through into the world wearing his own physical body: it could only come through in essence, and then had to kill and take over a human body, to move around in the world. Perhaps that's why she couldn't remember how to defeat a demon in its natural state. Maybe she'd never had to before. It was only because this demon had discovered a weak spot between the worlds that he could appear in his own form. A form that was now reversing the angel into a wall to crush her and force her to let go of his shoulders.

Dread smashed her into the wall again and again, until finally Saraf was forced to release him, and drop to the ground, bruised and exhausted.

'Well, well, well,' said the demon, prodding her with his foot. 'This is a first. An angel protecting an imp. Why is that, I wonder?'

'You were being cruel,' replied Saraf, 'I don't like cruelty.'

This answer made no sense to the demon, who only found pleasure in inflicting pain, and exercising power over others.

'You don't expect me to believe that, do you?' snarled Dread. 'There must be a better reason. So why don't you want me to kill my own imp? Is it that drinking his blood might increase my strength? No, I've got it! You're afraid that he can lead me to this girl ... the one with the special blood. Of course! But in that case you'd want me to kill him. Was this some kind of pathetic rescue attempt, so that you can take control of him, or is this some sort of double bluff?' The demon leaned over her, his rank breath making her choke.

Saraf couldn't begin to answer, partly because she could hardly breathe and partly because she couldn't make sense of the demon's way of thinking at all. She had just wanted to rescue a creature in pain and fear. The idea of a double bluff, or even a single one, was beyond her.

'I don't like cruelty,' Saraf repeated.

'What a shame,' grinned Dread, maliciously. 'Perhaps we need to broaden your experience. I doubt if you've ever suffered at the hands of an expert. Allow me to educate you.' Grasping her shoulder with one hand, and the base of her wing with the other, Dread began to wrench the muscles apart, and Saraf found herself weeping with pain and fear.

Glint crouched on the ground watching. He felt perhaps he ought to interfere because the angel had been trying to rescue him but he was an imp, after all. Nobody could expect him to behave with any kind of decency. He was just glad that the angel was the one getting hurt and not him. He decided to take the opportunity to escape and began to crawl along the ground towards the exit. He knew it would be too dangerous to try and return to the Darkness just then. Suddenly he found his route blocked by a pair of large, sandaled feet, half hidden by the bottom of a long, white gown. The imp lifted his head up. And up. This angel was much taller than the other one. And much scarier.

The imp found himself being hauled up into the air, yet again, and carried back along the tunnel towards the spot where Dread was trying to pull the wings off the smaller angel.

Fen took one look and used the only weapon he had to hand to try and protect Saraf: the imp he was clutching. He used all the force he had and flung the imp directly at the demon.

The impact made Dread let go of Saraf as the imp bowled him over. Dread got back on his feet preparing to fight, but the smaller angel was trying to stand up too and the new arrival looked ready for battle, while the demon was already tiring.

Besides, he didn't want to get distracted. It was more important to find the girl with the special blood.

Deciding that on this occasion discretion was the better part of valour, Dread grabbed Glint and held onto him as the demon leapt over the barrier and into the cave marked Inner Temple, making for the spot where the Darkness and the world touched. The last glimpse the angels had of Glint was of his terrified face as Dread dragged him back into the Darkness, as his prisoner.

8

Saraf looked up at Fen, relief flooding her face, but before she got a chance to express her thanks, he was shouting at her.

'What in heaven's name did you think you were doing?' roared Fen, furious, 'Getting into a fight with a demon. You could have been torn apart.'

'I'm sorry,' whispered Saraf, close to tears. 'He was being cruel to the imp. I was just trying to stop him.'

'It's not our job to defend imps,' said Fen, a little more gently. 'They can look after themselves. We're supposed to look after people. What are you doing here, anyway?'

'I followed the imp back from the accident,' Saraf explained. 'It was the imp that caused it.' Saraf explained what she had learnt about Glint drinking Phoebe's blood and causing the accident. 'I don't think he meant to hurt them.'

'I don't care what he meant to do,' growled Fen. 'He put her and her fiancé in hospital, and now there's a demon who knows that there is something special about her. Who'll be trying to find her. What a mess! And you were trying to stick up for the imp?'

'He was being hurt. It wasn't … *kind*,' muttered Saraf, stubbornly. She shook as she stood up and Fen reached out a hand to steady her. She looked as if she was in considerable pain, and her robe was ripped across the shoulder, when the demon had tried to wrench her wing out of position. Some of her feathers were bent out of shape, where her back had been smashed repeatedly against the wall, and there was a bruise forming on her cheek.

Fen supported her as they walked up through the tunnels to the outside, stopping for Saraf to catch her breath when they reached the courtyard.

'How did you find me?' asked Saraf, as they locked the door to the tunnels on their way out.

'I followed your trail in this direction, and then flew around looking for anything odd. The gates being open after hours at a place called The Hell-Fire Caves was a bit of a clue. Plus, once I was close enough, it was as if I could sense you.'

'That's nice,' Saraf smiled for the first time since finding the crashed car. 'Perhaps you like me a little. It would be lovely to have a friend.'

'Don't get carried away,' said Fen. 'With my track record any friend of mine is likely to end up in trouble. You're better off just being an associate.'

Saraf nodded, sadly. Much as she wanted - needed - a friend, she knew she couldn't force someone to be friends with her. Although perhaps she could keep trying.

'How's your girl?' she questioned, once they were outside the main gates to the caves.

'I don't know,' replied Fen. 'I left her at the hospital and came looking for you.'

'Then you should get back there,' said Saraf, firmly. 'I'll come with you. Now a demon knows about her, it's bound to take both of us to keep her safe.'

Fen looked at the childlike angel, already damaged from her battle with Dread, and wondered how much help she was going to be. Then he remembered that it was down to her curiosity that they knew that the accident wasn't an accident, that an imp and a demon knew that there was something special about Phoebe, and that they were aware of the location of a weak spot between the world and the Darkness.

'Can you still fly?' asked Fen.

'Let's find out,' replied Saraf, with a grin.

She had found it difficult to manoeuvre in the air, and the pain was intense, but she had done it. Saraf felt like she'd flown a hundred miles, not just about thirty, by the time they reached the hospital. Saraf wasn't sure how much help she'd be able to give Fen until her body had had time to mend, but before she could say anything, he was hurrying through the corridors to where he'd last seen Phoebe and Marco.

They arrived in a large room full of medical equipment, just as a nurse was pulling up a sheet to cover Marco's face. Phoebe, who had recovered consciousness, was howling in grief. The sound cut through both angels' hearts, but there was nothing that they, or anyone else could do to help the young man. He had died from the natural consequences of the car crash, and not even angels could change that. Even if the crash itself had had a supernatural cause.

Fen felt familiar waves of guilt being to wash over him as 'What Ifs' rolled around his thoughts. What if he'd reached his new charge sooner? What if he'd realised there was an imp in the car, could he have prevented the accident? Grabbed the creature, thrown his own body between the young man's head and the windscreen, or the roof. Saraf grabbed Fen's hand and squeezed it tightly, to interrupt the whirlwind of doubts and regrets in his head. If anyone was aware of how well a guardian angel can do guilt, it's another guardian angel.

'You couldn't have stopped this,' she whispered. 'You went to her straight away. The accident had already happened. You have to stay strong so that you can help her now. She's going to need you, with a demon after her blood.'

Phoebe recklessly pulled the tubes out of her arms and scrambled down off the trolley she'd been lying on, dragging a blanket with her and struggling to keep her balance as her feet touched the ground. She staggered over to where Marco's body lay, and flung her arms around him, while the nurses tried to make her return to her bed for treatment. The medical staff whispered to each other hurriedly and two nurses took hold of the ends of Marco's trolley and started to wheel him out of the room, while another draped the girl's blanket around her shoulders as they gently pulled Phoebe away from her fiancé's body.

'You'll get a chance to say goodbye properly later, dear, but for now we need to treat you,' said the young doctor.

'I don't care,' cried Phoebe, 'I don't care about me ... I just need to be with Marco.'

'But it's not just about you, is it?' said the doctor softly, steering her back towards her bed, and helping her onto the trolley. Phoebe nodded weakly, dropping the blanket she'd been clutching as she used both hands to climb into her bed. The doctor picked it up and laid it gently over her, but not before the angels had got a good look at the girl's stomach and realised they were now trying to protect not one life, but two. Fen groaned. He'd never been great with babies.

9

Phoebe woke up in a hospital bed. She was no longer in the resus unit, but had been moved onto a ward. She remembered nurses talking around her, coming to check up on her. Slowly she began to remember other things … things that ended up with the image of Marco lying still on the trolley beside hers, before his face was covered with a sheet.

As waves of grief washed over her, Phoebe began to sob, and endless thoughts chased each other around her brain. Why did Marco have to die? Why not her? If only they'd never gone to the caves. Or could afford a newer, safer car. Why now? Why not after the wedding? The honeymoon? A lifetime together?

She was overwhelmed with sorrow, and barely registered the doctors and nurses monitoring her. They were just a blur of figures in different coloured uniforms. Green, blue, white … not that she understood what the different colours meant.

A random thought imposed itself in Phoebe's troubled mind. She decided there should be a wall chart next to every bed, explaining who wore which colours. She thought that the white was a bit impractical. It was such a brilliant white. Surely it would show every bloodstain, or splash of vomit. The other colours made more sense. The figure in white seemed to be there most often though: it wasn't a doctor. But then, she didn't need that much medical care, did she? Lulled by the pain relief a nurse had injected into her, Phoebe drifted back into sleep.

The next time she woke she could hear voices nearby. No. One voice. Talking quietly. But it was like listening to one end of a telephone conversation. The person was obviously speaking to someone else, but Phoebe couldn't hear their replies.

Not that what she could hear made much sense.

'One of us needs to go back to the caves, and find a way to seal off that section. The one the demon vanished through … or heaven knows what we'll have to deal with.'

'I'm supposed to be here … keeping watch.'

'Of course you can remember what to do. Just think about it.'

'You can't have forgotten everything.'

'No, don't get upset. I didn't mean to make you feel bad. I just … I need you to … all right … don't panic. I'll go, and you stay here and watch over her. Better?'

'Good.'

The voice was gone, and the next time Phoebe woke up she thought she'd imagined the whole thing. Either that, or someone nearby had been listening to a very peculiar radio play.

Back in the Darkness, Glint quivered with fear as Dread shoved him into a small cage. The imp could barely fit into it, and although he tried to remain silent when Dread wrenched one of his arms out through the bars and wrapped a chain around it, he found he was whimpering. Next the demon grabbed the imp's other arm and chained it to the other side of the cage.

'There,' said Dread, maliciously, 'That'll stop you escaping … nowhere to hide now. Not in the world and not in the Darkness. So you can just stay here and think about what I'm going to do to you when I get back. In the meantime, Imps, come here. Now! Let's see what verminous little creatures are around.'

An assortment of imps scuttled forward, some small, some scaly, all ugly and twisted.

'Ah,' said Dread, sighing in satisfaction, 'Excellent. You lot torture this creature. You used to know him as Glint but now he's just a prisoner. One who needs to be taught a lesson. I want information from him about a human girl. One who has …' Dread stopped himself before he could finish the sentence. The last thing the demon wanted was for any other creatures of the Darkness knowing about the girl with the strange, powerful blood in her veins. 'One who I need to find. Fetch me when he's ready to speak.' Dread turned on his heel and went to think, which he found easier without the distraction of the sounds Glint was making as the other imps try to 'persuade' him to talk by raking him with their claws, biting him, burning him with hot iron pokers.

After an hour or so one of the imps came to find Dread. The creature crouched before the demon nervously, wringing its clawed hands.

'Glint doesn't know,' it whispered. 'Not who, not where. He'd have told us … can't tell us what he doesn't know.' Dread was furious. Partly because what this imp was telling him made sense, but it wasn't what the demon wanted to hear.

'Name,' snapped Dread. The imp in front of him squirmed. All the Lesser Invisibles knew that it was safer to be as anonymous as possible, especially where demons were concerned.

'Name,' repeated the demon, more loudly.

'Snig,' whispered the imp.

'Well, Snig,' said Dread, menacingly, 'Go and try again.'

'But …' Dread kicked the little imp hard enough to lift him into the air and send him some distance back towards the cage where Glint was held.

'Torture him again,' the demon called after the imp, as the creature scrambled back onto its feet and returned to its fellows crowded around the imprisoned Glint.

After several more hours of torment it was apparent, even to Dread, that Glint was unable to give him the information he needed. Reluctantly the demon released the imp from the cage.

'You're coming with me,' Dread announced. 'You'll help me find the girl. Then I'll bring you back and return you to this cage to await your punishment.'

Glint groaned, feeling he'd already received as much punishment as he could take, but Dread took no notice. Instead he dragged the imp along by the neck and then hurled him towards the weak point between the worlds.

Snig watched from the shadows, surprised to find himself feeling some kind of sympathy for his fellow creature. He told himself it wasn't his problem. After all Glint didn't even look much like a normal imp anymore so he wasn't really one of them. But still, curious, he followed the brutal demon and his captive.

Fen found himself before the High Council for the second time that day. He needed help to report the weak spot between the worlds. He had never heard of such a thing before and wanted advice on how to seal it. Unfortunately, it turned out that none of the angels on the High Council knew exactly what to do either, but one of them did have an idea.

An angel called Celeste suggested that Fen needed to work out why the weak spot was in that place, what had been done to open it, and then attempt to do the opposite. It was as near to a plan as any of them could come up with and she and another angel from the High Council agreed to accompany him to The Hell-Fire Caves if they were needed, to help him seal the entrance to the Darkness, once he'd figured it out.

Meanwhile, rumours about what Dread was doing had been spreading. The imps who had been assigned to torture Glint had no loyalty to each other, or to the demons, and saw no reason to keep their mouths shut about what Dread was up to.

Before long, half a dozen other demons knew that he was looking for a girl with 'special' blood which could turn an imp into Something Other. In which case, what might it do to a demon? And why should Dread be the only one to get the benefit? The other demons began to follow Dread, creeping behind him in the Darkness looking for the way through into the world. A way which didn't require any rules to be broken, or invitations issued. A weak spot that was just there in the Darkness, waiting for them.

10

Fen had left Saraf to watch over Phoebe. He knew it was supposed to be his job, but he was also absolutely certain that the weak spot in the caves, where creatures from the Darkness could get through, needed to be dealt with as quickly as possible, before the demon who'd escaped through it came back looking for Phoebe.

He'd have preferred to send Saraf to sort out the problem, but she'd become agitated when he asked her to, claiming she couldn't remember what to do, and in the end he'd given in, and agreed to leave her at the hospital, while he went to find a solution to what was going on in The Hell-Fire Caves.

When he arrived, it was still the middle of the night, so he knew there wouldn't be any people around. He landed in the centre of the courtyard and saw at once that they had a problem. The gates into the tunnel system were bent out of shape, and one was torn off its hinges, as if something had forced them open from the inside.

Fen froze for a moment, trying to assess the risk to himself. To Phoebe. To Saraf. He guessed that the demon they'd fought with earlier had come back but hopefully the creature wouldn't know exactly where Phoebe was, which might give him a little time. Torn between hunting for the demon, when he didn't know where to start, and investigating the weak spot in the caves, he chose to hurry down into the tunnels, to see if there was anything obvious that was providing the link into the Darkness, some way he could stop more creatures coming through.

When he reached the Inner Temple, Fen saw an assortment of dummies, dressed as members of The Hell-Fire Club, their servants and companions, in eighteenth century clothing. Some of the figures were standing and some were seated around a small table covered with replica food and drink, wax fruit, goblets, flagons of wine and candle sticks. Fen examined everything closely but couldn't get a sense of anything wrong Perhaps there was an artefact that might be creating a link to the Darkness? At the back of the cave was a statue, again harmless. Beside it was a huge jar, over three-foot tall, and in the space between the two objects. There it was – a sense of disturbance. Something not quite right.

Fen realised what it was: someone, a long time ago had made sacrifices here. Though Fen wasn't sure what of. Surely not human? Perhaps animal sacrifices, over and over again, in an attempt to invite 'something' from the Darkness into the world.

Whether some of the members of The Hell-Fire Club, if that was who it had been, were successful at the time, Fen didn't know but it felt as if repeated sacrifices, and attempt after attempt to invite something through had created the weak spot that was now allowing creatures from the Darkness through into the world without a specific invitation.

Fen had hoped he'd find some artefact that was the cause of the problem, something he could just destroy but what he'd found was more complicated. The weak spot was woven into the fabric of the caves, and he didn't know what to do to alter it. He was going to have to go back to the High Council and accept their offer of help. Perhaps they could come up with a solution? Although with the demon having come back through already, it might be a little late to fix the problem. Still, one demon should be manageable so long as the High Council could find an answer before any more escaped into the world.

Fen made his way out of the caves and once he reached the courtyard he took to the air, winging his way towards the High Council. He suspected that they'd be unimpressed with him coming to them for yet more help less than twenty-four hours after receiving his new assignment, but there was nothing he could do about that.

Saraf sat on the end of Phoebe's hospital bed, kicking her heels against the bedframe … She was bored. The angel had been keen to stay and watch over the injured girl and even more keen not to have to revisit the caves and deal with the demon again, but all Phoebe seemed to do was sleep. Given the amount of sedative she'd been dosed with, this was hardly surprising, but from Saraf's point of view it did make things a bit dull. Although, she had to admit, dull could be good. It meant the human she was watching over was still alive, and there weren't any nasty demons or imps about causing trouble. The bored angel didn't know yet that Fen had discovered something had already come through from the Darkness. Something that was going to make life anything but tedious.

Fen had led Celeste and the team selected by the High Council to the place in the caves where the weak spot was. He was a little puzzled that as well as a couple of angels the team had included two humans: a young male minister called James Frankham, and an older woman, Pamela Martindale, who practically glowed with belief in *Him*. Fen had never realised that on occasion, to prevent certain types of incursions from happening, not just angels but Christians could go into battle, when prayer and faith were needed. Shocked at what this implied about humans and angels being able to communicate in some circumstances, Fen watched as the humans worked with the other angels to identify the vulnerable spot and used prayer, and Holy Water to cleanse the ground previously defiled by sacrifices and incantations, and build up a sacred space that was as unwelcoming to the creatures of the Darkness as the weak spot had been inviting. They finished by embedding a silver alter cross, laid flat on the ground directly over the location of the trouble spot.

'Won't some human working in this exhibit just kick that out of the way?' asked Fen eventually, allowing himself to be seen.

The older woman chuckled and got a plastic ice cream tub out of her handbag. He saw that it was filled with a dry mixture of sand and cement.

'Not once we've fixed it into position,' she said, and proceeded to fetch a little water from the stalagmite pool and mix it into the mortar. Once it formed a thick paste she passed the tub to the minister saying, 'Here, you can crawl around down there to cement the cross in place. My knees aren't up to it.' The young man quickly spread out the mortar and laid the cross on it, pressing it down until the mixture oozed up around the metal.

'That should do it,' said James, getting to his feet. 'Now if we just spread a little earth over the top. There. No-one will ever know we've been here.'

'Except the demon,' laughed the woman. 'I think he'll notice a few changes. Well now that's done, I need to head home. A cup of tea and a good night's sleep, that's what I need.'

'There's not much night left,' said James, 'but our job is done.' After a final blessing of the site, the mismatched pair left the caves and Fen approached the other two angels.

Celeste was tall, taller than Fen, with long red hair, twisted into a ponytail to keep it out of her face, and penetrating dark green eyes. Despite the traditional white robe she was wearing, she seemed very modern and business-like, and Fen could see why she was on the High Council. The other angel, who was called Able, was even taller, with dark skin and tightly curled black hair, starting to turn golden at the tips. This had the disconcerting effect of making Able look as if he had a halo. His robe was sleeveless, revealing arms that looked strong enough to snap even the most powerful demon in two. Fen felt like a wimp in comparison to these two.

'Who are they?' Fen asked Celeste. 'Why didn't you try to remain invisible? We're meant to be discrete and you were both talking to them. Working with them.'

'They're the second line of defence,' she responded, 'When we can't do certain tasks on our own, we call on people of faith.'

'We have faith!' protested Fen.

'No, we don't,' Celeste answered, 'We have knowledge. It takes humans to have faith ... to believe in what they can't see.'

'You let them see you!'

'They both had faith long before that,' said Celeste, smiling, 'Look, we've called on them for help before. We started out being very ... circumspect. Remaining invisible, trying to influence them indirectly and so on ... But after a while they realised what we were anyway, and it just became quicker to approach them directly. Especially in an emergency.' The angel looked sheepish. 'Of course, there were a few consequences to that. We broke the rules by telling them and created an imbalance. As a result, a demon came through and had to be dealt with. But once a human knows, they know. There's no point in pussyfooting around them after that, and speaking of humans, hadn't you better get back to yours? As far as you know you've got a demon, or some other creature from the Darkness, on the loose and looking for her, you shouldn't leave her alone.'

Fen considered explaining that Phoebe wasn't alone, he had Saraf looking after her, but since Saraf working with him hadn't been arranged or approved by the High Council, and he wasn't in any case sure just how much use she would be, he decided it was quicker to head straight back to the hospital. He was thankful that with the gateway into the Darkness sealed off, he'd just have one demon to cope with.

He was wrong.

11

Dread was hiding in the shadows of the hospital car park. This was the third hospital he'd dragged the imp to, since Glint's sense of direction was poor, and he hadn't paid much attention to which way the ambulances had driven off after the accident.

Dread was growing increasingly frustrated. He'd have liked to rip the imp into tiny pieces, but the demon needed his help to identify the girl. Also, he was aware that Glint would be a little harder to destroy than most imps, now that the girl's blood had increased the creature's size and strength slightly. Something else was worrying Dread too: it was nearly morning.

On any previous opportunities the demon had had to enter the world, he had come through in essence and had then had to take over a human body, one way or another, in order to have a solid form he could control, and use to interact with other humans, as he tried to steal their soul-lights. That was always the primary aim of a demon, to come out of the Darkness and into the world to collect as many human souls as possible. The more they could take back into the Darkness with them when they were eventually forced to return there, the more powerful they became in their own dark hierarchy.

Usually they could only come through if rules were broken. Rules that held the two worlds in balance. If humans found out too much about the presence of Angels among them, or the existence of the Darkness, of Demons or Lesser Invisibles like imps, then a demon would have the opportunity to enter the world. Even then, they would still have to wait for some foolish human to actually invite them in, deliberately or by accident. According to the rules the person who invited the demon across was the only person the demon had the right to attack. Not that demons were particularly bothered about sticking to the rules.

However, on this occasion it seemed to Dread that there

were no rules at all. He had come through into the world wearing his own demonic body and he wasn't sure what would happen to that body if he abandoned it here to take over a human. Even if he could find a way to do it. Which meant he would be wise to remain in his demon form, but that had disadvantages. Any human seeing him would likely run, very quickly, in the opposite direction. Unlike Lesser Invisibles demon bodies weren't invisible, though some people might just ignore them or dismiss them as someone wearing a rather good fancy dress costume. Humans were good at disbelieving the testimony of their own eyes if what they were looking at didn't make sense to them.

Dread knew he'd have to remain in hiding during the day, and before that happened, he wanted to locate the girl with the special blood.

As he had done at the other hospitals they'd tried, Dread sent Glint in to scout around. After all, the imp would be able to recognise her, while Dread would not. Glint was reluctant to be sent on yet another fruitless search but a little senseless brutality from Dread soon persuaded him.

The imp slipped into the hospital and started searching. He couldn't find any trace of the girl in the Emergency Department, so he crept up stairways and along corridors and eventually noticed something odd. He felt a tingling sort of sensation as he approached a bed in one of the wards. This bed had the curtains closed around it, to give the patient some privacy and when he sneaked beneath the curtains to take a look, he saw the girl he was searching for, asleep in the bed, and sitting on the bottom of the bed, with her back to him, was an angel. The angel who had followed him to The Hell-Fire Caves. The angel who had unexpectedly stood up for him.

Glint ducked back beneath the curtains and hurried out to the car park where Dread was waiting for him.

'She's there,' confirmed the imp. 'Up in one of the wards on the third floor, but it won't be easy to get to her now. She's protected.'

'What do you mean?' the demon demanded.

'There's an angel watching over her,' Glint replied. 'One of the ones from the cave. If she's got her own guardian we'll never be able to get to her.'

'Oh, we'll get to her all right,' muttered Dread. 'It'll just take a bit more planning, that's all.'

With that, the demon dragged Glint out of the carpark, searching for somewhere to hide for the day. So that he could think, and make plans.

When Fen returned to the hospital, he was relieved to find that Phoebe was sleeping and Saraf was watching over her.

'Nothing's happened,' Saraf complained, unaware that the imp had located the girl. 'It was really boring.'

'I'll take boring,' said Fen. 'My night was ... weird. The High Council sent a couple of humans along with two angels, to seal that gateway. They all worked together. It was ... strange.'

'Humans?' Saraf was amazed. 'How could they involve humans? They're not supposed to know we exist, are they?' Fen shrugged, and sank down into the chair beside the bed.

'That's what I thought, but it seems I was wrong. For some things, angels need humans. Well, certain humans, anyway.'

Saraf turned to look at the girl sleeping in the bed. 'What do we do now?' she asked Fen.

'We wait, I suppose,' he replied. 'When she wakes up, she'll be in quite a state, with her fiancé dead, and we'll have to make sure she doesn't do anything foolish and protect her from that demon, if he finds her.' Fen settled further down into the chair to get some rest, unaware that the demon had found Phoebe already.

Just as Dread and Glint had searched for Phoebe, the six demons who had followed Dread through into The Hell-Fire Caves before the gateway was sealed, were searching for him. After all, if Dread had come through into the world in search of a girl with special blood, whatever that meant, they wanted some of it too... Or in fact - all of it. Once they'd used Dread and the imp to locate the girl, they wouldn't need him anymore and without him, there would be more blood for the six of them to share.

12

Phoebe stirred. The curtains had been drawn back from around her bed, and sunlight was flooding the ward. For a moment she lay there, confused, enjoying the sunshine in a distant, hazy way. Then the memories washed over her, and she began to shake. One of the nurses rushed over, and took her hand.

'Now then, Phoebe, just lie still. You've been in an accident. You're all right. Just a bang on the head and a few cuts and bruises.'

Phoebe's hand instinctively moved to her stomach, and the nurse added, 'Your baby is all right, too. The seatbelt kept both of you safe.'

Phoebe looked at the nurse, wondering how to ask about Marco. She thought she remembered but hoped it was just a bad dream. The nurse saw what the girl was thinking and felt she needed to hear the truth.

'I'm afraid your fiancé wasn't so lucky. His injuries were more severe, and although everyone here did their best, I'm afraid we couldn't save him. I'm so sorry.'

Even though Phoebe remembered seeing Marco in the emergency department - could still see the sheet being pulled up over his bruised, bloodied face - she had clung to the hope that it was just her imagination; some kind of waking dream. Now that hope was gone and so was Marco. All she had left of him was the baby she carried. She sank back onto the pillows, silent tears flowing down her face, and for a while the nurse just sat with her, holding her hand.

Eventually Phoebe asked, 'How long to I need to stay here? I have things to do. I have to let people know about Marco, and cancel the wedding. It was ... next week. I suppose I'll need to arrange his funeral too ... Oh my god. It's real. He's really gone ...'

Phoebe's breathing became ragged as the truth overwhelmed her.

'For the moment, all you need to do is rest,' said the nurse sympathetically. 'The doctors will be along soon to check you over. If they're happy I expect they'll let you go home today. They kept you in to monitor you, and the baby. Do you have anyone we can call for you?'

Phoebe shook her head. Marco, and the passion for painting that they had shared, had become her whole world over the last three years. After graduation the week before, most of their mutual friends had scattered though half a dozen had been due to return for the wedding. Phoebe's parents were both dead. Her mother had died of cancer just before Phoebe began her art course, and her father of heart problems a couple of years later. To Phoebe it seemed that her father had died of a broken heart, he had missed her mother so much. Now she knew how he felt. Without Marco she was bereft, with no one to talk to, or to run too. The young couple had been so wrapped up in each other and the future that they were building together, that they'd drifted away from the friends they'd made before they'd started their courses, and never really spent that much time with their fellow students. Now Phoebe had nobody to turn to.

Marco had been in much the same position. Parentless since he was a young child, he'd been raised by his grandmother in Rome, before travelling over to England to study. She thought he'd mentioned a couple of cousins, once or twice, and the best friend he went to school with, the one who'd been going to fly over to be his best man, but the only relative he was close to was his grandmother.

The awful thought came to her then - she'd have to phone his grandmother and tell her Marco was dead. Silent tears slipped down her cheeks. This was just too awful. She could barely face it herself. How would a frail old woman take the news? Phoebe thought her heart would break.

Fen and Saraf looked at each other helplessly. Phoebe felt

completely alone, though she wasn't, not while she had them watching over her. But she didn't know that, and they couldn't tell her - not without breaking the rules, and they had enough trouble to deal with already, without allowing more into the world.

It was late afternoon by the time Phoebe was discharged from hospital. She was clutching a bag of Marco's personal belongings, and was given a lift back to their flat in Bristol by a hospital transport minibus. She felt guilty, as she wasn't really ill, but the hospital staff had insisted that it would be better for her and for the baby, if she could be taken straight home, and not have to manage on public transport, or worry about finding money for a taxi, just then. Their kindness was almost too much to bear, and she couldn't help crying as she thanked them. Despite Marco's death, the hospital felt like a warm, comforting cocoon, in stark contrast to the empty flat she'd be returning to.

She climbed into the hospital minibus, giving the driver her address as she did so. Hidden around a corner of the building, Dread smiled. He'd been wondering how to follow her home, keeping her in sight without being seen. Now he didn't have to. He could just wait until it was fully dark, and make his own way there when he was ready. He saw the two angels boarding the minibus behind her, and smiled to himself. If those two tried to interfere in his plans, which they were bound to do, he would take great pleasure in destroying them, as well as their charge. In fact, he was rather looking forward to it.

Dread turned to see Glint trying to slip away, and reached out a long, clawed arm to prevent the imp from escaping. His talons dug into the creature's skin as he twisted Glint's arm, harshly.

'You don't need me now,' whimpered Glint. 'You've seen the girl; you know where she lives. Let me go.'

'Oh no,' said Dread, 'Not yet. I might need you. Anyway,

you still have to be punished for keeping secrets. Besides, I can't let you go. You might tell some other demons about the girl. Then they'd come after her. There'd be less blood to go around. And I can't have that, can I?'

Of course, Dread didn't realise that it was too late to worry about that. Some other demons had already come through from the Darkness, searching for the girl. They hadn't found her yet, but they had tracked down Dread, and the imp he'd dragged along with him. By the time these creatures had located Dread and Glint, Phoebe, along with the angels who were protecting her, had already left.

One of the demons, a hideous dark green creature called Drear, lunged forward, eager to attack Dread on the spot. Collecting human soul-lights gave a demon power, but so did killing a fellow demon, while in the human world, and he was keen to try.

'No', said another of them, known as Daunt, grabbing Drear by the arm and holding him back, 'Not yet. If you attack him now, we can't use him to find the girl'. Drear tried to wrench his arm free from Daunt's grip, keen to escape from his fellow demon's sharp talons.

'Daunt's right,' agreed another demon, called Dire, and two of the others sniggered - it was rare for demons to agree on anything.

'All right,' growled Drear, 'If you insist, we'll wait and follow Dread when he leaves. But when we no longer need him, I get first shot at him'.

'I don't think so,' said Dire, bristling so the spikes on his head stood up even more sharply. 'It'll be each demon for himself, when it comes to it - Just like always. But for now, we need to be clever. We'll wait for Dread to move and he'll wait for darkness. Better for all of us not to be seen by humans in our natural forms.'

'There are six of us,' argued Drear, 'We can tackle a few humans if they spot us.'

'We wait!' hissed Dire. 'Concentrate on finding the girl. Then we can share her blood between us.'

'Then can we kill Dread?' Drear demanded.

'Then we can kill anyone we choose,' Dire replied. 'This is going to be fun!'

The other demons chuckled in agreement, but it wasn't the kind of laughter that made you want to join in; more the kind that chilled you to the bone and made you look for somewhere to hide. Somewhere a long, long way away.

13

Phoebe let herself into the flat and slumped down onto the sofa. She leaned back and closed her eyes for a minute wishing she could drift off into sleep. She just wanted to forget for a few moments, but her brain was filled with things she had to do. All her wedding planning lists were scattered across the table and she knew she had to start cancelling the arrangements as quickly as possible. Perhaps, under the circumstances, some people wouldn't charge the full fee for their services if she let them know at once. Not that Phoebe was usually focused on money, but she knew she'd need to pay for Marco's funeral and the baby was coming soon. She reached out for the wedding lists, then reluctantly she picked up the address book instead.... She had another, even worse task ahead of her. Phoebe needed to tell Marco's grandmother that he was dead and call his best friend, Giovanni, who was due to fly over for the wedding.

Feeling helpless, Fen and Saraf watched as Phoebe spent several difficult hours on the phone, informing such friends and family as they had that there wasn't going to be a wedding after all. The worst call was to Marco's grandmother. Phoebe dialled the number and introduced herself, and then struggled to find the words.

'Nonna Battista. I'm afraid I have bad news for you. About Marco. He's ... there was a car accident. I'm so sorry,' Phoebe could hear sobbing at the other end of the line, 'He's dead.'

'My Marco?' said the old lady, ''e is dead?'

'I'm so sorry,' said Phoebe, struggling not to start weeping again herself. 'It was very quick, the doctors said. He wouldn't have been in pain.'

Phoebe was trying to say anything she could think of to comfort Nonna Battista, and found herself wheeling out phrases from medical dramas, all the time wondering where the words were coming from. She didn't know if Marco had suffered or not. She couldn't bear to think about it. She just knew that Marco would want her to soften the blow as much as possible. To protect his beloved grandmother from distress, as far as she could.

After a few minutes the old lady pulled herself together, choking back her tears.

'And you, Phoebe?' she asked. 'Are you hurt? And de *bambino*?'

'I'm all right, just a bit bruised. They wouldn't have let me out of hospital if I wasn't ok. The baby wasn't hurt either. Just Marco. I'm so sorry. I know he was like a son to you. I … I don't know what to say …'

'At such times there are no words. Take comfort in de *bambino*. In de love you shared with Marco. I wish I could come to you, bring you strength, but I am not well myself. If I was able, I would have come to de wedding. Now,' Nonna Battista paused, another sob escaping her, 'Now I will not be able to come to 'is funeral.'

The conversation left Phoebe in tears and Marco's grandmother told her to go and get some rest but she couldn't. Phoebe knew she wouldn't be able to sleep until the first, worst job of letting everyone know, was completed.

Phoning Giovanni, Marco's best friend and best man, had been tricky. He was with the Italian police force and had been difficult to get hold of. When she finally reached him., his voice was brisk and professional. He didn't sob like Marco's grandmother, he just sounded - stricken - and confused. Phoebe found herself waffling on about plane tickets and hoping he could get a refund, and feeling like a total idiot, until eventually the silences between them became so long and awkward that being able to say goodbye and put the phone down was a relief.

Each time she made a call and had to explain to yet another person that Marco was dead, it felt like being punched in the stomach. Forcing herself to say the words over and over was a nightmare but in some ways, it made it more real too. There was no use in pretending to herself that it was all a bad dream, or a mistake, and that Marco would come charging in through the door at any moment, filled with excitement about some new idea for a piece of art he wanted to create.

He'd never be able to create anything again. That was the hardest thing for Phoebe to absorb.

Once she'd made all the personal calls, she started contacting some of the people involved in the wedding. The caterer and the photographer both worked from home, so she called them before it got too late. Each of them was kind and sympathetic, and said not to worry about any fee. It was all Phoebe could do not to cry with relief. They'd only planned a small wedding at a registry office, with about a dozen guests, and a simple buffet afterward in a pretty local pub by the river. It seemed to have taken ages to plan, but undoing the arrangements took barely an hour. Even the manager of the pub was kind. She and Marco had been in a few times to make the arrangements, and he seemed more upset about the accident, and Marco's death, than he did about cancelling the hire of the room for the reception.

With just the registry office left to contact in the morning, Phoebe finally felt that there was nothing else she could do that night. A wave of exhaustion washed over her and she allowed herself to relax for a moment. Curled up on the sofa she drifted in and out of a troubled sleep. Strangely, she felt she could hear a voice again, the one she'd heard in hospital, but she was too tired to open her eyes and see who was speaking.

'There's no point in both of us keeping watch.'

'No, I'm not. You're welcome to stay; I'm just saying you don't need to.'

'They'd have to find her first, and how are they going to do that?'

'All right, stay then, if that's what you want,' said the voice, sounding exasperated.

Phoebe opened her eyes. She couldn't see anyone in the room, there was just a kind of … whiteness in one spot. She glanced around to check that she hadn't mindlessly put the television or the radio on but no, they were both switched off. Perhaps the sound was filtering in from the flat next door, that must be it.

She's wished they'd either turn the programme down, or turn it up enough for her to hear both halves of the conversation. Just hearing one side of it was giving her a headache. The room went quiet again and Phoebe sighed with relief.

Eventually she decided she'd be better off going to bed, rather than falling asleep on the sofa. She stood up, and glanced around the little living room. Everywhere her and Marco's paintings were hung on the walls, or leaning against the furniture. Hers were mostly landscapes, full of colour and light, expressing a joy in life and in the world around her. Phoebe doubted that she'd ever feel like creating anything joyful again.

Marco's works were dark and gothic. They showed his fascination with everything fantastical and macabre, with death and decay, although some of them were strangely beautiful too. They were a complete contrast to his positive, enthusiastic personality. The only exception was a small canvas on which he'd painted a portrait of Phoebe, when they'd first got engaged. It showed her at her best, and he had painted it with such love that even Phoebe could imagine she was beautiful when she looked at it, although most of the time she considered herself ordinary looking.

Phoebe wandered into the bedroom and pulled out her wedding dress, which was wrapped in a sheet to stop Marco from seeing it. Feeling drawn towards it, Phoebe took it out of its cover, and took a final look at it, then broke down in tears, as the realisation hit her, yet again, that she would never get to wear it. Perhaps the shop would take it back since it had never been worn. Another job for the morning. She hung up the dress and sank onto the bed.

This time she fell into a deep sleep.

Fen and Saraf had been taking turns to look out of the window, and watch for any sign of trouble that might appear in the street. They had reasoned that the demon could only find Phoebe if he'd tracked her to the hospital, and followed her home from there, and the longer they waited in the flat without an attack happening, the more they began to relax.

'What do you think of your new charge?' Saraf asked as she turned away from the window to look at Fen. 'Is she interesting? Are you going to enjoy protecting her?'

'I suppose so,' replied Fen, thoughtfully. 'A girl with angel blood being chased by a demon ... That's definitely interesting. But I'm not sure that I'm the right guardian for her ... not with my track record. She seems so ... vulnerable.'

'You're worried about her?' questioned Saraf.

'I suppose so.'

'But that's good isn't it? It means you care what happens to her,' Saraf smiled, 'That's an improvement on the last person, isn't it? If you can feel something for her?'

Fen shrugged. 'I don't know what I feel at the moment. I don't really know what she's like. I wish I could have seen her before all this. She's so stressed now that it's hard to judge.'

'Well,' said Saraf, smiling, 'Maybe that's why you've been sent to her. You know all about stress.' Fen gave her a hard stare, wondering how much she knew about his past, and the way he'd fallen apart after the earthquake, but Saraf just smiled innocently, and started humming a little tune to herself.

'Look at the paintings,' said Saraf, suddenly excited as the thought struck her. 'If you want to know what she's like, look at her work.'

Fen realised that Saraf was right. They were surround by pictures, and artists don't just paint to decorate a room, they put their hearts and souls onto the canvas. Fen started to inspect Phoebe's work, and Marco's. They were so different to each other and Phoebe had obviously been so full of optimism before the accident.

Fen was just beginning to get a sense of what Phoebe was normally like, how she saw the world, and deciding he liked what it showed him of her, when the door to the flat burst open and Dread appeared in the doorway.

14

Fen and Saraf were horrified. The creature was big and ugly and was slavering in his enthusiasm to rip the angels to pieces and get to Phoebe to take her blood. Fen realised at once that instead of sitting about waiting for the demon to attack they should have been preparing themselves for the battle.

Usually items that humans considered holy had some power over demons. Crosses, icons and Holy Water would be very useful. Fen looked around for these things now. He could have kicked himself for not taking the threat seriously ... for not being ready. He'd become used to protecting humans from everyday hazards, or failing to. He'd forgotten how to fight a demonic battle.

Saraf, to Fen's surprise, was better prepared. From around her neck she pulled out an intricately carved metal cross, which she wore beneath her gown. Holding it out in front of her she marched towards the demon, thrusting it into his face. The creature screamed and backed away, but only for a moment. Then he swung his heavy fist into her face, sending her flying across the room.

As the demon turned to concentrate his attention on Saraf, Fen charged at him, grappling the creature to the floor.

'You can't come in here,' Fen shouted, 'You don't have the right. She never invited you into the world.'

'She may not have,' growled Dread, struggling in Fen's grasp, 'But some human did, repeatedly, to form a gateway between this world and the Darkness. I'm just exploiting what's already there.'

Saraf had landed against the coffee table, shattering its glass top, and scattering the things that had been on it across the floor, including an unlit scented candle. She scrabbled around for the box of matches that she'd noticed earlier, and lit the candle. She advanced towards Dread, who was still wrestling with Fen. They were too evenly matched for either of them to win against the other.

'Saraf, I could do with a little help here, please,' groaned Fen, as Dread grabbed him by the throat and squeezed. Saraf thrust the candle close to the demon's face, and the creature tried to turn his head away from the light.

'The light shines in the darkness and the darkness cannot put it out,' intoned Saraf gleefully, as with her other hand she placed her metal cross against Dread's forehead. It was too much for the demon, who couldn't draw strength from his right to be there, for he had no right. Saraf's words and the intensity of the flame being used as a symbol of heaven, and the painful contact of the cross with his skin, coupled with Fen's strong grip pinning him down, meant that Dread knew he couldn't win this battle without help.

'Glint,' the demon commanded. 'Get in here.'

The imp however, was cowering on the landing outside Phoebe's front door, wondering why the demon expected his help, when all Dread had done to him for hours was torture and threaten him. In fact, Glint suddenly realised that this was his chance to escape from the demon, and started to run away. Seeing that the imp was deserting him instead of jumping into the fight, Dread gave a sudden twist to his body, loosening Fen's grasp and wrenching himself away from the cross and the candle. Free, but defeated, for the time being at least, the demon turned and fled, catching up with the fleeing imp as they both ran down the stairs, and taking him prisoner once more.

Bruised and battered Fen hauled himself to his feet: he hadn't taken that kind of a beating in years. He really didn't feel up to this job. Saraf blew out the candle and ran to him to see if he needed any help. Suddenly a voice made them both jump.

'What's going on?' said Phoebe, standing in the doorway

to her bedroom. 'Who are you? And what was that ... *thing*?' Saraf and Fen looked at each other in horror. Now they were for it. Angels weren't meant to be seen. Ever.

Phoebe was staring at them, clinging to the doorframe for support. She was ghost pale and shaking, having witnessed such a scene on top of all the other shocks the last day or so had brought. Fen admired the fact that the girl was still standing and not succumbing to hysterics. Both angels started fluttering their wings at the right frequency to be invisible to humans, and vanished from Phoebe's sight.

'What do we do now?' asked Saraf in a panic.

'I'm not sure,' replied Fen. 'Maybe she'll think she just imagined us.'

'And the demon?' queried Saraf.

'I expect so,' said Fen. 'Nobody believes in demons, these days, or in angels. She'll probably put it all down to a bad dream, and have forgotten about it by the morning.'

'SHE won't do anything of the kind. I saw you, and I can hear you. One of you anyway. I heard you before, at the hospital and here too. So it's no use pretending you're not around,' said Phoebe, with more determination than she really felt. 'Show yourselves.'

Saraf shrugged, and stilled her wings, and a moment later Fen allowed himself to become visible too. He reasoned that if Celeste, and the other angel he'd met that night, could appear to James and Pamela once they knew of their existence, what further harm could it do if Phoebe could see them?

Phoebe took in the sight of two rather different angels, one older male and a young female. Both traditional looking, and each appearing to be rather hot and bothered after the fight.

'And the other ... thing?' asked Phoebe.

'Gone,' answered Fen. 'We fought it off. For now, anyway.'

'For now?' Phoebe repeated. 'That doesn't sound good.'

'It isn't,' agreed Fen, 'And talking to you will only make things worse.' This was true enough. Allowing themselves to be seen definitely broke the rules, which were about balance and counterbalance. Whether talking to the girl would allow some Lesser Invisibles to come through from the Darkness, or give Dread more right to attack her, Fen didn't know. But he was pretty sure it would be a good idea not to identify Dread as a demon, for the sake of Phoebe's sanity.

'You're all right,' said Saraf chattily. 'We drove the demon away. I expect he's gone back to the Caves, and returned to the Darkness. So, you'll be safe now.'

Fen groaned. 'No, he can't have done. We sealed the gateway so no more could get through. The demon is trapped here.'

'And it might come back?' challenged Phoebe.

The angels nodded, embarrassed. They felt that between the two of them they ought to be able to keep the girl safe but they had barely managed to tonight.

'Why did it come here, anyway? To our flat? I mean ...' Phoebe's voice trembled as grief sunk in again, 'to my flat?'

Fen glared at Saraf, hoping she realised that whatever else Phoebe found out, they could never tell her what made her so special. Knowing that would almost certainly put her in even greater danger, and things were bad enough already.

15

The other demons had tracked Dread and Glint to the house where Phoebe had her flat. They didn't know exactly which part of the building she lived in, but they would easily be able to narrow it down and find her. Which meant that they didn't really need Dread anymore. They watched as their fellow demon hurried out of the building, looking rather burned and frustrated, dragging the squirming imp along with him. Having lost the fight, Dread was happy to take his rage out on Glint. They gathered around the struggling pair, sneering and hissing, until Dread stopped beating up the imp and turned to face them.

'What are you doing here?' Dread growled, horrified to see them.

'Just looking,' said Dire.

'Following you,' said Daunt.

'We heard you'd found one of Eskarron's descendants, and we want a share of the blood,' stated Drear. The other three demons grabbed Glint, and started pulling the imp's limbs this way and that, causing pain, as demons loved to do. Especially when bored. Glint squealed, but none of the demons took any notice.

'She's mine,' growled Dread.

'Not by invitation,' said one of the demons. 'You have no more right to her than the rest of us. She didn't invite you into the world.'

'She didn't invite anyone,' ventured Glint, nervously. 'Nobody invited nobody.' All the demons turned to stare at him. The imp gulped and corrected himself, 'Anybody ... nobody invited anybody.' The demons continued to stare at him. It was not reassuring.

'NOW you become talkative?' said Dread. 'You stayed silent for ages, about the way into the world and NOW YOU'RE

TALKING?'

Glint tried to shrink into himself wishing that he hadn't swallowed any of the girl's blood. He'd be better off looking small and insignificant – but he couldn't do anything about that now. He had a feeling that all seven demons were about to turn on him and rip him apart and there would be no coming back from that.

Up in Phoebe's flat, the conversation wasn't going much better. Phoebe was demanding answers and there were too many things the angels didn't dare tell her.

'You mentioned the caves ... You said the creature, the demon ... it would go back there. Do you mean The Hell-Fire Caves?'

The angels looked at each other and nodded.

'So, it followed Marco and me from there?' Again, Saraf and Fen exchanged glances. 'So the accident?' Phoebe persisted, 'The car crash ... Marco's ... what happened to Marco ... Is that all part of the same thing?' Both angels looked at the carpet. 'And you let that happen?' They looked at her in horror. 'That's it,' announced Phoebe. 'Get out! I don't want you here,' and the girl turned and stormed into her bedroom.

Moments later they heard her weeping and looked at each other miserably.

'I don't think she likes us very much' whispered Saraf.

'You're probably right,' said Fen gloomily. 'And she's going to like us even less soon.'

'Why?' asked Saraf.

'Because we need to get her away from here, quickly.'

Dawn was breaking and the demons knew that they needed to get out of sight. It wasn't that daylight hurt them, it was just that if people got a good look at them ... well, it wouldn't go well. Of course if a single person came across them and over-reacted, they could more than defend themselves. In fact, they'd be fighting over who got to swallow that unfortunate person's soul-light.

Every soul-light collected and carried back into the Darkness increased the power of the demon that consumed it but if a large group of humans ran into them, who knew how that would end? At best it would distract them from capturing the girl.

For now, they needed to take shelter while they planned what to do next. The obvious place to return to was The Hell-Fire Caves where they could easily slip back and forth between the Darkness and the world. Or so they thought. After all, they knew where to find the girl now, they didn't need to keep watch during the day.

'We can come back tonight' announced Dread, trying to exert his authority of the group.

'If we all attack together,' agreed Drear, 'the angels would have no chance to protect her.'

It was settled; they could all come back after dark.

When Phoebe emerged from her bedroom late the following morning, she looked around the sitting room puzzled. All the paintings had been taken down off the walls and Fen was busy wrapping them up in brown paper and stacking them carefully in a large box.

'We thought you'd want to take these with you,' he muttered, not meeting Phoebe's eyes.

'To keep them safe,' Saraf added. 'A demon can be very destructive, if he's in a bad mood.'

'Which he will be,' finished Fen, 'When he comes back tonight and finds you've gone.'

'Gone?' said Phoebe weakly. 'I'm not going anywhere.'

'I'm afraid you are,' said Fen. 'We can't protect you here. We need to move you to somewhere safe.'

'But this is my home,' protested Phoebe, although she hardly wanted to admit to herself that it didn't feel like home anymore. Not without Marco. Without him she felt as if nowhere would ever be home again. 'I have things I've got to do …' her voice petered out. Everything she needed to do was about Marco's death.

'We'll help,' said Saraf, brightly. 'You need to have something to eat, and then help us pack. Two piles. Things to travel with, and things to keep safe in storage … in case it takes a while.'

'In case what takes a while?' asked Phoebe, as Saraf practically shoved her into the kitchen to have some food.

'Getting rid of the demon,' answered Fen wearily. 'Until we do that you and you baby won't be safe.'

An hour later Phoebe had had some breakfast, rather reluctantly, and dressed. She packed a suitcase of her own clothes and at the last minute added a favourite jumper of Marco's, that still smelt of him. She was struggling to grieve with everything else that was going on around her, and that seemed the hardest part: not having the freedom to break down completely. She added a few personal possessions - her own and Marco's - to her case, and looked around the room. Most of what was left were clothes that had belonged to Marco, and her wedding dress. She had wanted to take it back to the shop, but the angels were insisting that there wasn't enough time. She ran a hand over the beautiful creamy fabric one last time, sighing for the broken dreams it now represented, then carried her suitcase into the living room, closing the bedroom door behind her.

'Have we missed anything?' asked Saraf. She had been the one who'd insisted that they didn't just whisk the girl away without giving her a chance to prepare herself and salvage some of the things that mattered to her. The things that reminded her of Marco. Things that might be lost if the demon came back and trashed the place.

'Paintings and photographs are in that box,' Saraf continued. 'Small things and your paints and brushes are in that bag … you'll want them with you.'

'How long will I be gone?' whispered Phoebe in horror, looking around the stripped-out room. Only the books remained in place, and a few other possessions that were too bulky to pack. The sitting room looked alien to her now.

'We don't know,' said Fen solemnly, 'But you won't be able to come back until you're safe. I don't want to take any chances.'

'You already did, didn't you?' said Phoebe. 'If you were supposed to be protecting us, where were you when we were in the caves? When we had the accident? When Marco died?'

Fen couldn't look Phoebe in the eye, as feelings of guilt and failure washed over him again. Rather to his surprise, Saraf leapt to his defence.

'He wasn't your guardian angel then. He wasn't assigned to you until after some of that happened,' she announced. 'So it's not his fault. He's doing his best. So am I … we're just trying to keep you and the baby safe, so don't get angry with him.'

Phoebe sank onto the sofa, her legs shaking. She couldn't handle any of this. Until yesterday she hadn't believed in angels or demons. Or even God. She wasn't quite sure she did now, to be honest, and here these strange creatures were, taking control of her life. She couldn't get her head around it at all. She knew that Marco would have found all this fascinating, and loved every moment of it, but Marco wasn't there anymore.

The doorbell rang and the angels exchanged glances, nervously, then Fen pulled himself together.

'Don't worry, Phoebe,' he said. 'Demons don't use doorbells.'

'Probably,' added Saraf, unhelpfully.

Phoebe opened the front door and was amazed to find a young man in clerical clothing standing in the doorway. Fen, who'd made the arrangements, hurried over to introduce them.

'Phoebe, this is Reverend James Frankham. I thought we might need reinforcements.'

16

The rest of the day passed in a bit of a blur for Phoebe. Her possessions were loaded into James's car, and he drove her to the registry office to cancel the wedding and record Marco's death. Phoebe pulled the medical certificate the doctors had given her out of her shoulder bag, and handed it over to the registrar, who was so kind and gentle about her loss that the girl could hardly complete the formalities.

It was a relief when everything that needed to be done was finished and they were back in James's car.

'Now what?' asked Phoebe, exhausted, settling her bulging body into the passenger seat. 'I can't go back to the flat tonight, and I don't have the money for a hotel.'

'It's all right,' replied James. 'You're going to stay at the vicarage tonight. It's in Stow-on-the-Wold, although if that doesn't suit you, a lady called Pamela Martindale would be happy to put you up. She's one of my parishioners.' Exhaustion overcame Phoebe on the drive to Stow, and she only woke up as James turned the car into the drive of the vicarage. Before her was a small, modern house, built of the local Cotswold stone. The soft honey colour of the brickwork gave the house a welcoming air.

'I thought vicarages were vast, rambling old places,' muttered Phoebe, struggling to get out of the car.

'They were,' laughed James, as he came around to help her out, 'but the vast rambling places tend to be sold off to raise revenue, and the clergy get moved into houses that are smaller, more practical, and easier to heat.'

James quickly got Phoebe's bags and boxes into the house, putting them in the small room he used as a study, then carried her suitcase up to a guestroom. Phoebe kicked off her shoes, lay down on the bed, and fell asleep again within minutes, her arms wrapped around Marco's jumper, breathing in the reassuring smell of him. With all that was going on this was the only way the girl could cope. Fen and Saraf were glad that she slept whenever she could.

'Well,' said James to the two angels looking out of the windows of his sitting-room, 'What do I need to expect, and when?'

'Trouble,' replied Saraf, brightly.

The demons had made their way back to The Hell-Fire Caves early that morning, only to find that their way back into the Darkness had been blocked. The spot in the Inner Temple that had been Glint's way in and out of the Darkness for longer than he was prepared to admit to Dread, was no longer usable. Each of the demons tried to look unconcerned, but secretly they were worried. The normal rules didn't seem to apply now they were trapped in the world in their demonic form, and none of them knew how they'd be able to return to the Darkness, once they were ready too. Only Glint, however, gave any sign of being alarmed, squealing and moaning and finally irritating Dread so much that the demon started to kick and punch the smaller creature. The other demons joined in, happy to have an excuse to lash out and vent their frustrations on someone.

By the time they'd finished Glint was a trembling, broken mess on the floor of the cave. The demons left him there, having decided to hide in the woodland behind the courtyard of the Caves until dusk, when they would make their way back to Phoebe's flat.

Once they were out of sight, and before any human visitors arrived, Snig crept out of hiding. He had followed Dread and Glint through from the Darkness the day before, and instead of trailing the rest of the demons, when he saw them appear, he had stayed around the caves. He had seen the gateway between the two worlds being closed and had spent the night working out how to cause a little enjoyable mischief when humans were about. Before he got the chance to put any of his ideas into action the demons had returned, and Snig had opted to stay hidden. Watching how they treated Glint, he felt he'd made the right decision. Now he reached out and prodded the battered imp lying before him. A faint groan was enough to encourage him to drag Glint out of the Inner Temple and into the River Styx, moving him to a place around a bend in the river where the two of them were hidden from view.

Snig wasn't sure why he felt compelled to help his fellow imp: Lesser Invisibles were hardly known for kindness or compassion, but seven demons beating up one imp didn't seem fair. Whenever demons got angry, they always seemed to take it out on the imps, as if the only way they could make themselves feel better was by making someone else feel worse. Usually someone smaller and weaker and Snig had had enough of it.

The trouble was, Snig wasn't sure what to do next. He wanted to get back to the Darkness and take the injured imp with him if he could. But he didn't know how to get there. Usually imps came through in their physical bodies, just as he had, and were driven back by prayer, or being sprinkled with Holy Water, or just being physically kicked out of the world and into the Darkness by an angel ... but he didn't have access to any of that. Or did he?

Phoebe didn't wake up for hours, until the dusk of the long summer evening was gathering outside the vicarage. She hauled herself upright and looked around the unfamiliar room. Each time she awoke she wanted to believe that everything that was happening to her, and what had happened to Marco, was a dream. Each time she realised more quickly that it wasn't. Even her bruised and aching body served as a reminder.

The last couple of days had been completely surreal, with the visit to the caves, the car accident, and Marco's death seeming almost normal compared to the other things that had happened since. Creatures she didn't even believe in attacking her, protecting her, dragging total strangers into her life. She decided it was time to pull herself together and to take back control. How could she stay in the house of someone she didn't even know? And why was she imagining all of this? It must be some weird form of shock and that was hardly good for the baby. She made her way downstairs feeling a little refreshed, and ready to dismiss her imaginings and ask the vicar to take her to a train station so she could go back to her flat in Bristol.

As she approached his sitting room, she could hear voices, and thought that perhaps one of his parishioners had come to visit him. She knocked politely on the door, and then opened it to find that she was right. The vicar was chatting to an older lady, who turned and smiled sympathetically at Phoebe when she entered the room. Side by side on the sofa sat the two angels.

'Oh,' said Phoebe, disappointed. 'I thought …'

'You thought you'd imagined us?' stated Fen, flatly.

'You hoped we'd have disappeared by now?' added Saraf, looking sad. Nobody likes being disbelieved in, and for Saraf, who seemed to have been alone ever since 'her boy' died, hundreds of years ago, it was disappointing to feel unwanted when she was trying her hardest to help … and connecting with people and other angels for the first time in centuries.

Phoebe nodded guiltily.

'Don't worry, dear,' said the older lady, who James introduced as Pam. 'You have had rather a lot to deal with lately, from the sound of things. I'm so sorry to hear about your young man and the other troubles you've been having. But never mind, the worst is over now. You'll be safe here.'

Having held it together all day, Phoebe cracked and found herself sobbing uncontrollably on the shoulder of this kindly stranger, while Fen and Saraf exchanged looks. They weren't at all sure Phoebe was safe yet. All they'd done was bought her some time.

17

Snig was waiting impatiently for the humans to go home. He'd realised that hiding in the caves wasn't going to get them back to the Darkness, not now that the gateway between the two worlds had been sealed ... But he'd also realised that as imps, he and Glint did have more than one way back, unlike the demons. Snig just needed to find the right materials ... and he was anxious to go looking for them. Especially because he feared the demons would return soon, for want of anywhere better to go, and if they caught him, he'd probably end up like Glint. He certainly didn't want to sit around and wait for that to happen.

Cursing the fact that long summer days meant he couldn't go searching for hours, Snig tried playing a few simple tricks on the human visitors to the caves. Normally he loved the opportunity to come through from the Darkness and cause a little chaos, but his heart wasn't in it that day. He was too concerned about returning to the relative safely of his home before he ran into any more foul-tempered demons.

When darkness came he crept out of the caves and began to explore his surroundings. The caves had woodlands behind them, which covered a sizable hill. He decided to climb to the top to view the local area and see if he could spot what he needed. Uncertain if the demons had left the woods, he moved with caution, trying to be as silent as possible. When he reached the top of the hill, he found a huge, castle like structure, which, on closer inspection, turned out to be a mausoleum. Tucked beside that was exactly what he'd been looking for: a church. He was relieved because he had thought he might have to walk miles to find one.

It never occurred to him that the door might be open, that churches welcome visitors. Instead he picked up a rock and smashed a small glass window. The act gave him the first moment of real pleasure he'd felt all day because any act of destruction was a delight to an imp. He scrambled up the wall and in through the window, finding himself in the vestry of the church. The vicar's robes were hanging on a hook opposite him, and for a moment he was tempted to put them on and dance around in them but what was the point when there were no humans there to see him and be afraid?

Feeling rather uncomfortable in the sanctified atmosphere, Snig went into the main body of the church. Being unfamiliar with the inside of a church building he shivered with nerves.

'Hello?' the imp called out, 'Anyone here? Any angels? I could do with an angel ... just this once. I want to get home.' The was no reply. 'Typical! The first time I actually want to meet an angel, there isn't one. Oh, well, I'll have to figure it out for myself then.' He wasn't exactly surprised. His previous contacts with angels hadn't exactly ended well. Whatever made him think one of them would come to his rescue?

Wandering around the empty church the imp's skin began to itch. He really didn't belong there, and he knew it. He felt like running away, but first he needed to find what he was searching for. He reached the baptismal font and hauled himself up to look down into the water. Tentatively he dipped the tip of one clawed finger into it.

'Oooow! That hurts! Not fair.' The imp was squealing and hopping up and down. He'd found what he was looking for all right! Holy Water blessed by a minster and touching it was agony.

When the pain subsided Snig crept under a pew to think. He hated Holy Water. It burnt him when it came into contact with his skin and angels used it to sprinkle onto imps to drive them back into the Darkness. It wasn't a pleasant way to be sent home but it did get you there quickly. So now he had two choices. One was to dive straight into the water in the font. The pain would be intolerable, but he'd be back in the

Darkness in seconds. The second was to find a container, fill it with Holy Water and carry it back to the caves to sprinkle on himself and Glint, so they both got home. It did seem like an awful lot of effort though!

Phoebe was feeling a little calmer, having cried out some of her misery and fear on Pamela's shoulder. James had made them all hot chocolate. Well, all the humans, anyway. Angels didn't need to eat and drink although Phoebe did find it a little disconcerting when Saraf came over and sniffed her drink and then smiled.

'That's wonderful,' said the angel. 'It smells so good. Can I have one?' Fen glared at her, but James just passed her his cup, content to humour the young angel. Saraf sat sipping it in delight as the conversation swirled around her.

'I need to organise Marco's funeral,' Phoebe was saying, miserably.

'I can do that,' James said, kindly, 'But you do need to decide what you want.'

Phoebe looked at him, puzzled.

'Well,' James continued, 'Was he a Christian? A member of any faith or church? Would he have wanted to be buried or cremated? Do you want a big service or a small one? That sort of thing.'

Phoebe felt inadequate once more. So many questions and she wasn't sure she knew the answers. She knew he was a Catholic, and his love of everything gothic meant he'd possibly prefer to be buried, rather than cremated, if she could afford it but that was as far as she could get. It was Pamela who suggested phoning Marco's grandmother, to see what she thought. She was the closest that the young man had had to a mother after all. While the girl went out into the hallway to use the landline, the other four looked at each other.

'How bad is this likely to get?' asked Pamela. 'You said the demon was likely to come after her?'

'It'll be bad,' acknowledged Fen. 'Phoebe has … something this demon wants and he won't stop until he catches up with her and gets it.'

'How exactly will he get it?' questioned James.

'He'll rip her apart and drink her blood,' said Saraf, trying to lick the inside of her cup. 'Have you got any more of this? It's delicious.'

18

Led by Dread the demons had broken into Phoebe's flat and were disgusted to find no trace of the girl, or the angels. They began to search the place for any clue about where the girl might have gone and being demons, they didn't search tidily. The art books and other possessions that Phoebe had left behind were shaken, torn apart and thrown on the floor. The crockery was smashed and the cushions ripped open. Although that was more about the pleasure of wonton destruction than because they actually expected to find information inside a cushion.

One of the demons, Drool, was searching the bedroom and came across the wedding dress, carefully wrapped up inside the wardrobe. The creature immediately tried it on, his sickly yellow spital staining the pale fabric. He began prancing around the flat pretending to be a blushing bride, until the others, their tempers frayed by the girl's disappearance, turned on him and ripped the dress to shreds, taking some of the flippant demon's skin off with their claws in the process.

Eventually there was nowhere left to search, and the demons were none the wiser. 'Now what?' asked Drool, staring at the others resentfully, his skin still sore from their bad-tempered attack. 'We can't follow the girl, she's disappeared. We have no way to find her and share her blood and we can't get back into the Darkness. What are we going to do next?'

Dread glared at him, turning an idea over in his mind before replying.

'Perhaps there is something we can do. There is still one clue we can follow. That pathetic imp, Glint, he drank some of her blood and they do say blood calls to blood. Perhaps he can find her for us.'

'Or his blood can,' said Dire, chuckling.

James was looking at the angels suspiciously. On several occasions in the past Celeste had called on himself and Pamela to help deal with something from the Darkness, in an emergency, but generally that sort of contact with angels was fleeting. He wasn't used to having them chatting in his sitting room and drinking hot chocolate, and he still found it rather remarkable. He did wonder why Saraf had a rip in her gown, up at the shoulder, but didn't like to ask though he guessed it wasn't a fashion statement. Even so, he couldn't imagine her getting into any battles: she looked so harmless.

'There's something you're not telling me, isn't there?' asked the vicar, staring at both the angels.

'Yes,' replied Saraf, cheerfully, wiping her sticky mouth of the back of her sleeve. Fen nudged her with his foot, trying to shut her up.

'We can't tell you,' Fen explained apologetically. 'It's not allowed and it's not something you need to know. Just accept that the demon is after her, specifically, and he isn't going to give up.'

'So, what can we do?' asked Pam. 'There must be a way to keep her safe?'

'Yes, of course,' agreed Fen. 'I just haven't figured out what it is yet.'

At that moment Phoebe walked into the room looking shell-shocked.

'What is it?' Saraf asked as she jumped to her feet and went to stand beside the girl, taking her arm to support her.

'It's Marco's grandmother,' said Phoebe, numbly. 'She wants me to take Marco ... his body I mean ... to Rome. She needs him to be buried there.' She sank into a chair saying 'How on earth am I supposed to arrange that?'

'I can help with that,' James reassured her. 'It's difficult, and expensive. But it can be organised'

'She says she'll pay for it,' whispered Phoebe, 'If I can organise it.'

'Leave it to me,' said James firmly then he glanced towards the angels. 'What do you think? There's no reason not to send the body to Rome, is there?'

'I suppose not,' said Fen, turning the idea over in his mind. 'In fact, it'll be even better if Phoebe goes with it. The demon is hardly going to go and look for her there.'

'That's settled then,' Pamela announced. 'Now, you look after the arrangements, James, and I'll look after Phoebe. Oh, and have you got a needle and thread in the house? Saraf's robe needs mending.'

Snig spend the best part of an hour arguing with himself. Could he really be bothered to carry Holy Water all the way down to the caves just to help some other imp get back to the Darkness? After all, there wasn't anything in it for him and it wasn't fun, which were the only two factors that mattered to an imp. They certainly didn't do friendship.

On the other hand, he was fed up with the way the demons bullied and beat up the imps whenever they felt like it. Rescuing Glint might just annoy the demons, which would be a plus. Then again, annoying demons did tend to have consequences… Painful consequences. Was it really worth it?

Snig crawled out from under the pew and wandered around the church looking for a container to carry the liquid in. In a cupboard in the vestry he found a silver chalice, but when he went to pick it up contact with such a sacred item hurt, so he abandoned the idea and used an old tea cup instead. He found it remarkably difficult to climb out of the vestry window with a teacup full of Holy Water, and couldn't help spilling some of it painfully onto his claws. Carrying it down through the woods and into the caves was tricky too, but when he reached the back of the cave system, he realised that after all that effort, he was too late. The demons were back and they'd found Glint.

19

Snig tucked himself out of sight, to listen to the demons' conversation.

'Well, Glint, my loyal little imp,' Dread was saying, 'You drank some of her blood. Is it telling you anything? Giving you any clues about where the girl might be?'

'At the flat?' gasped Glint, weakly. 'Isn't she there?'

'If she was there, we wouldn't be here,' growled Dread, annoyed. 'She's missing. Those angels have taken her somewhere, and we need you to find her.'

'But I can't,' cried Glint, anxiously. 'I don't know how.'

'Then we might as well kill you now,' said Dread, with relish, 'Since you're no use to us.'

'No, wait,' whimpered Glint. 'Give me a chance... Perhaps I can ... sniff her out, or something. Only don't kill me.'

'Show us what you can do then,' snarled another demon. Snig didn't dare get close enough to work out which one it was, 'And start now.'

Snig tucked himself further into a crevice in the tunnel as the demons began to drag Glint though the caves to the surface. For a brief moment Snig considered trying to rescue the other imp, by rushing out of hiding and throwing Holy Water over Glint and himself. In theory that would drive both of them straight back into the Darkness, leaving the demons trapped in the world, but he was a coward. There was too much that could go wrong, like only having enough left in the teacup to send one of them back. After all, he had split rather a lot of it on the way. In the end he decided Glint wasn't his problem after all, waited until he was alone in the caves, and poured what was left of the Holy Water over his own head.

'Owwwwwwww!' Snig screamed as it burnt his skin, causing him to almost pass out with the pain. When he opened his eyes, he was relieved to find that he was back in the Darkness, safely home. Well, not entirely safe - a demon was kicking him in the head.

'Get moving,' the creature said, hauling the imp to his feet, 'You've got work to do.'

Phoebe was still struggling with the idea of burying Marco in Rome - well, of having to bury him at all. Two days ago she had been looking forward to going there for their honeymoon and now it was to lay his body to rest in the soil of his homeland. She already felt exhausted and overwhelmed by everything that had happened, especially when she was so far through her pregnancy. She reached down beside the chair, and lifted up her shoulder bag, digging around in it to find the papers Marco had given her. The plane tickets were still in there, along with a piece of paper that she hadn't looked at when he first gave it to her. It turned out to be a list Marco had written: all the places he planned to take her on their painting trip - not just Rome but Sorrento, Pompeii, Herculaneum: he had wanted to show her his country, and he had it all planned! Now she'd be going there with his body. He wouldn't be able to introduce her to his grandmother - Nonna Battista - they'd have to meet over his coffin instead. What a terrible thought! Phoebe struggled not to burst into tears again: she'd done enough of that lately. She had a fiancé to bury and a baby to prepare for. As difficult as this was going to be, she had to be strong for her child's sake.

Across the room, Fen watched with pride as the girl tried to pull herself together. In an attempt to give her some space, he was invisible again. Now her extreme emotions had settled, Fen could see Phoebe's soul-light was silver and it brightened a little as he watched. It would be a long time before she would be happy and at peace again, but Fen was beginning to think that she would get there eventually. She was stronger than he had first thought. All he had to do was protect her from the demon that was after her blood and that shouldn't be too difficult, especially if she went to Rome for a while.

James walked into the sitting room, carrying two mugs of coffee, and handed one of them to Phoebe. He was followed by Saraf, who increasingly liked the young vicar. He was practical, as well as kind. His smile was wide, his hair was reddish and even his soul-light, which was a warm yellow with touches of orange in it, suggested to her that he had a lot of optimism.

Of course, Fen could only see Phoebe's soul-light; that was how it worked. Angels could only see the soul-lights of the people they were responsible for, and he was just there to protect the girl. Saraf knew that meant she couldn't see Phoebe's, but was surprised she could see James's, and Pam's, which was a rich green in colour.

Saraf wasn't responsible for them, or for anyone, but perhaps no-one was protecting these individuals, and that's why she could see their soul-lights. She did wish the High Council would give her someone of her own to protect soon, it had been so long. Pam entered the room with a mug of coffee for herself, and a plate of biscuits – round ones with jam in the middle. Saraf began to wonder what they tasted like, if they were anything like as nice as hot chocolate. She reached out a hand to take one and saw Fen glaring at her from across the room. *Spoilsport,* she thought.

Fen sighed. Having Saraf assist him wasn't much help at all, she was so easily distracted. Still, she seemed to have been lost in grief for such a long time, perhaps it was good she was taking an interest in something. Even if it was just a plate of Jammie Dodgers.

'I've been thinking,' said Pam, 'There ought to be some kind of service for Marco here, before you go. It would give any friends in this country a chance to say goodbye and I think it might help you too, Phoebe, to face the journey ahead.'

Fen approved of the idea, after all, they couldn't move Marco to Rome immediately, there were formalities to deal with, which would take a few days. In the meantime, Phoebe was in that horrible stretched out stage between the death of a loved one, and actually being able to say goodbye properly. Fen allowed himself to become visible and smiled at the woman, to show his approval.

Phoebe nodded weakly, wondering how she'd face another round of phone calls.

'I'll help,' said Pam, 'Just make me a list of who to invite.'.

Fen could see that Pam was one of those admirable woman of a certain age, who held communities together, always pitching in and getting on with the tasks nobody else wanted to tackle. She was neatly turned out, with smartly waved grey hair, and had an almost timeless quality about her, but her most noticeable attribute was her kind and open expression. She was a woman who supported rather than judged, lived her faith, and believed in doing the best she could for the God she firmly believed in, and for everyone around her.

Phoebe found that Pamela reminded her a little of her own mother. The thought was oddly comforting. The angels, however, were rather more unsettling.

'Are you sure you're just supposed to hang around with us?' she asked Fen. 'Doesn't it cause more trouble? I thought you weren't supposed to be seen.'

'We aren't,' agreed Saraf. 'Not normally.'

'Perhaps if you'd just seen us for a moment, when we were fighting off the demon, we might have got away with it,' said Fen. 'You would have thought you'd imagined it, and you'd have talked yourself into thinking that it was a dream but you could hear us too.'

'Just you,' Phoebe corrected. 'I couldn't hear Saraf. Why is that?'

'I have no idea,' said Fen, firmly. He had a nasty suspicion that he could guess why. It could be because of Phoebe's angel blood. Different angels came from different flights, and he wondered if he was in some way related to Eskarron too … like Phoebe. But the whole angel blood story was one thing he was determined should remain a secret so he tried not to think about it too much.

'Phoebe does have a point,' said James, as he munched on a biscuit. 'Won't there be consequences? Of the two of you being so visible, I mean? I thought it was breaking the rules to appear more than necessary.'

'But this *is* necessary,' protested Fen. 'Phoebe is in direct danger from the Darkness. We need to be able to appear to her ... warn her ... to keep her safe. Anyway, if there were going to be consequences, wouldn't they have happened by now?'

'How do you know they haven't?' said Saraf, finally snatching a biscuit and nibbling on it. 'Something might be out there, right now, waiting to cause more trouble for us.'

'Like we need any more,' muttered Fen.

20

The demons were gathered outside Phoebe's flat, holding Glint captive between them.

'Now tell us,' demanded Dread. 'Where has she gone?'

'I don't know,' whispered Glint. 'How am I supposed to know anything?'

'You've shared her blood,' snapped Dire. 'There must be a connection. You just have to find it. *Have to* being the relevant phrase here ... if you want to live.'

'I can't feel anything,' hissed the imp. Three of the demons grabbed him and yanked his arm out of its socket. In his original form they would have pulled it off his body entirely, it was only Phoebe's blood enhancing his strength that saved him.

'You felt that, didn't you?' said Dread triumphantly as Glint moaned on the ground. 'Now get on with it.'

Glint reached out with his thoughts ... a bit of a stretch for an imp, as they were simple creatures who didn't generally need to exercise their brains. He couldn't actually smell anything, but if he tried moving in one direction, it actually made him feel less anxious than stepping towards anywhere else did. Perhaps that was it! Perhaps the girl's blood *was* calling to him. But he was pretty sure she wasn't nearby. If she was far way away, the demons would get impatient with him and rip him apart long before they reached her. Glint groaned, convinced that whether they found her or not, the night wouldn't end well for him. Still, all he could do was lead the demons towards the girl as well as he could, and hope things went better than he feared.

A hoard of Lesser Invisibles scattered around Stow-on-the-Wold in the middle of the night. The rules of balance and counterbalance had been broken when the angels became so casual about appearing to Phoebe, James and Pam, and as a consequence a number of imps had come through from the Darkness into the world. It would have happened more quickly if Fen and the others had stayed in Bristol, but breaking the rules and almost immediately relocating to the Cotswolds had confused the situation. So, instead of appearing near Phoebe's flat, where their mischief making might be a bit less noticeable, the imps were running riot in the quiet Cotswold town.

The first Fen knew about it was when he heard the sound of a car alarm going off outside the vicarage. He ran out to see if it was a distraction tactic caused by the demon, and discovered that there were imps spreading around the area causing trouble. Imps weren't a major problem of course, they weren't supposed to hurt anyone, and humans mostly couldn't see them, they could only see the results of their mischief. Still, Fen could have kicked himself. This was obviously the consequence of having broken the rules earlier, and now the angels would have to deal with it.

'Saraf!' shouted Fen, running back into the house, 'I need you to stay with Phoebe while I deal with some imps.'

'That's not fair,' said Saraf, sulkily. 'Dealing with imps is much more fun than staying inside. Why can't I help?'

'Because I need you to keep her safe,' muttered Fen, impatiently. 'Now please, just do as you're told.'

'You don't have the right to tell me what to do!' Saraf was indignant. 'You're not in charge of me.'

'True,' replied Fen, trying to be patient, 'But I do need your help, so please?'

'Oh, all right, I'll stay here with Phoebe but I'm not happy about it.'

Having settled that argument, Fen hurried to find the vicar.

'James, do you have any Holy Water handy? We've got a bit of a problem,' Fen called.

Outside the vicarage, crouched under the car, Snig

groaned.

'Oh no,' he thought. 'Not again.' This just wasn't his night.

Glint was leading the demons north and west, though he couldn't say exactly how he knew which way to go. Leading probably wasn't the right description either and mostly he was being pulled and pinched by his companions, which made picking out the correct direction even harder. If he couldn't find the girl he'd be ripped to pieces by the demons, and even if he could there was no guarantee that he'd get back to the Darkness in one piece. He was only leading the demons in her direction to save his own skin, but he was fairly sure that he was already a lost cause.

The journey took the whole night because not only did they have to travel a long distance on foot, but they also needed to stay hidden from view as much as possible, so they had to keep detouring off the main roads to take cover in the vegetation. As the sun began to rise, Glint groaned. He could tell that the girl was still some distance away, but they'd have to hide out of sight during the day. Breaking the bad news to the demons earned him yet another beating, which hardly surprised him, but hurt none the less.

As he settled down behind a hedge to sleep, he could hear the demons beside him, arguing over who had the most right to the girl's special blood and plotting what they'd do once they got back to the Darkness. They believed they'd be more powerful than all the other demons.

Glint turned his back on them, desperate to get some rest.

Fen and James had had a busy night. The imps had spread out across Stow-on-the Wold, causing mischief. Mostly they were a minor nuisance, snapping off car windscreen wipers, pulling up plants in gardens, setting off alarms and squashing their faces against peoples' windows to look scary. This last one wasn't as effective as the creatures would have liked since most people couldn't see them, and almost all the residents drew their curtains at night anyway. Lesser Invisibles didn't have the power or the right to hurt people, just cause a bit of trouble, and Fen and James had had to search the town, locating the imps one by one to get rid of them. Fen could just kick them straight back into the Darkness, James used prayer to send them home, and both used Holy Water sprinkled on the creatures to drive them straight back where they came from.

The imps were looking for people with extreme emotions, like anger of fear. These would give them more to work with - to exploit. However, it seemed that on that night, as least, the people of Stow were fairly content, and the Lesser Invisibles had to make do with simply causing a bit of malicious damage. Eventually things got back to normal in the early hours of the morning, and James and Fen returned to the vicarage to get some rest, hoping they'd got rid of all the Lesser Invisibles, though there was always a chance that they'd missed one or two. Which, of course, they had.

Snig found himself drawn to the churchyard. He had no desire to enter the building, but he liked the trees surrounding it, especially the two yew trees that grew either side of the North Door, their upper branches forming an arch. There was a narrow gap between each tree trunk and the wall of the ancient church, and it was into one of these gaps that Snig squeezed himself, planning to rest and stay out of sight until he could spot another opportunity to cause mischief.

21

Fen and James both looked exhausted when Phoebe came down in the morning. She wasn't much better herself, though she had been dealing with troubled dreams rather than troublesome imps. It was she who put the kettle on and made a round of drinks while James and Fen sat at the kitchen table too tired to speak, and Saraf sulked in the corner of the room because she hadn't been allowed to help battle the imps.

Pam breezed in a few minutes later, pulling several sheets of paper out of her handbag.

'I made a list,' said Pam smiling. 'Well, several actually.' She handed most of the pieces of paper to James and one to Phoebe.

'I went to the library this morning,' Pam added. 'I used their computer to check what needed doing for you to arrange to transport Marco's body to Rome, James. I've printed out everything you have to organise. The undertaker is going to collect the body… I mean Marco … from the hospital today and bring him here for the service tomorrow. As for you Phoebe, here are some suggestions for hymns and readings for the service here in Stow. And I've contacted the friends you asked me to invite. All but one of them can come, Sophie Alanson, but she sends you her love. I've booked the service time in the parish diary, Jean has offered to decorate the church with flowers, and Ivy will do teas afterward. I think that's everything, for now. Any tea in that pot? I'm parched.'

The others stared at each other in relief. Pam had already done most of a day's work before the rest of them had even had breakfast, and it lightened all their loads considerably.

Phoebe looked at the list of suggestions Pam had drawn up for her. Kindly she hadn't written down too many hymns to choose from, or readings. As someone with no connection to the church Phoebe wouldn't have known where to start, but Pam had narrowed it down to choices Phoebe could recognise, and she found she could make the decisions fairly quickly.

'I do hope Marco doesn't object to the service here being in an Anglican church; his burial in Rome will be Catholic. So long as James gets moving and makes the arrangements,' said Pam, looking pointedly at the vicar.

'They were up all night battling imps,' explained Saraf. 'That's why they're tired. And they wouldn't let me go with them. It's not fair.'

'Yes,' replied Pam, looking guilty. 'I noticed the imps. There was one under my car this morning. I'm afraid I didn't see it until it was too late ... I ran over it.'

'Good,' said Fen. 'One less to worry about.'

'I hadn't intended to kill it,' said Pam apologetically.

'You didn't,' said Fen. 'It'll just have vanished from this world and gone back where it belongs.'

'Thank goodness,' responded Pam, relieved. 'I know they're a nuisance but they're not as bad as demons. More like naughty children really. I'd hate to kill one by accident.'

'Imps?' questioned Phoebe. 'There are imps here?'

'Not any more,' said James, trying not to yawn. 'We've dealt with them.'

'We think so, anyway,' added Fen. 'There's nothing to worry about, Phoebe.'

They all knew that this wasn't exactly true, but it sounded reassuring, which was the best they could manage for the moment.

Glint woke up and gulped. The demons were standing in a semi-circle around him, prodding and poking his body. He tried to wriggle away from them but found himself backing into the hedge. He was cornered.

'What have you done?' growled Dread.

'Are you sick?' sneered Dire.

'No,' Glint replied, uncertainly. 'Why?'

'You're shrinking,' snarled Dread. 'The special blood you drank ... it must be wearing off.'

Glint gulped. Looking at his own body he could see that they were right. He wasn't back to his usual imp size, but he was heading that way. He didn't feel as strong as he had either.

'Which means you'd better help us find the girl fast, while you still have some kind of connection with her.'

'But it's daylight,' protested Glint. 'We can't move around in daylight.'

'*We* can't,' muttered Dire. 'But you can. Humans can't see you ... usually. Go and find her, and then come and fetch us when it gets dark and no slipping away back to the Darkness. We'll only make you regret it later.' Glint knew that this was true, and that there was no point in arguing with seven angry demons, so he scrambled to his feet and headed north west again, in the direction of Stow-on-the-Wold.

Snig was bored. He'd wandered around the town. There were lots of antique shops and places to buy fancy kitchen gadgets, and plenty of Japanese tourists taking photos. Snig had deliberately let himself be visible ... briefly ... in a few of their photos: that would confuse them when they got home and had their pictures printed. One or two of the tourists had new digital cameras. They were gathering their fellow travellers around them and chattering about the strange creature that was showing up in their shots. Snig scuttled away as the humans looked round wondering where the odd little animal had gone.

He went into a fancy tea shop and knocked over some nicely arranged piles of cakes, then stuck his nose in the book shop and carefully rearranged books on the shelves. It wasn't exactly full-blown evil, but it would certainly be annoying for the bookshop owners, and their customers. Early in the evening he strolled through the small town and found himself back in the churchyard. The trees and greenery struck him as calming; peaceful even. He rapidly shook off the feeling: imps didn't do peace. He saw something moving in the bushes nearby, another imp - of sorts. One that looked vaguely familiar.

Glint! What was he doing there?

Glint could feel that the girl with the special blood was nearby, as his body had begun to tingle again. He was relieved to have found her before he lost the ability to track her completely. He knew that the empowering effect of her blood was wearing off, and if he hadn't found the girl before it diminished altogether, and had had to return to the demons without that information, his last moments would be spent in agony.

Snig watched from the space behind the yew trunk as his fellow imp moved past the old church and headed in the direction of the vicarage. Snig climbed down and silently followed him.

22

Phoebe was in James's study sorting and repacking her boxes. James had offered to store the bulkier items like paintings, until she returned, so she was checking that nothing she wanted for the trip to Rome had been placed in the boxes with those. She boxed up some of her clothes too– she couldn't take everything to Rome and she would be coming back after the funeral. She pulled out a small photo album and decided to take it with her. That way she could show Nonna Battista the most recent pictures she had of Marco. Perhaps it would be a comfort to both of them.

As she flicked through the book, Phoebe didn't feel comforted at all. Each image reminded her of Marco and of everything they'd had, and planned and lost. Tears began to trail down her cheeks again. She no longer howled and screamed when she remembered him, the pain went deeper than that. Now her grief seemed more settled, sharper, wrapping her in silent isolation.

Glint climbed up and peered in through the study window, and saw her face crumpled with sorrow. A tiny part of him felt guilty. He remembered how she'd looked at the caves, before he'd tasted her blood, followed her … caused the accident. He brushed the emotion away.

Humans weren't his problem: angry demons were… And demons always seemed to be angry. So now he'd found her, all he had to do was go back to where he'd left Dread and the others and bring them to her. He scrambled down from the windowsill and found Snig waiting for him.

'What are you looking for?' asked Snig, curious.

'The girl,' replied Glint. 'The one who's blood made me special.'

'You don't look that special to me,' sneered Snig, 'You're

starting to look quite ordinary again.'

'I know,' replied Glint. 'The effect seems to be wearing off. I was afraid I wouldn't be able to find her, then the demons would have torn me apart.'

'They'll probably do that anyway,' said Snig. 'So why help them?'

'Because if I don't go back and tell them where she is, when we get back to the Darkness they'll torture me again.'

'I expect they will anyway,' said Snig, gloomily. 'Now that they've noticed you. You know what they're like.'

'I wish I'd never seen that girl,' whined Glint, 'Tasted her blood, killed her mate, any of it.'

'I expect she does too,' replied Snig, 'But you can't do anything now. The only way to help her is if … if you run away … don't go back to the demons or to the Darkness!' He was amazed that he could even come up with such an astounding idea but Glint dismissed it immediately.

'No way,' replied Glint. 'I'm not going on the run, hiding from demons forever, being stuck in this world. I'm going to get home, and the only way to do that is to give the demons what they want. HER.'

The front doorbell rang and James went to answer it. On the doorstep stood a dark-haired young man with a neat haircut, and green eyes. He was wearing a smart jacket and matching trousers, which was cut just too casually to be a suit. He smiled, nervously.

'Are you the Reverent James?' he asked, with a faint Italian accent. 'I've come to meet Marco's Phoebe. To help her. I am Giovanni.'

James opened the door and invited him in.

'That's wonderful,' said James, smiling. 'It'll be so good for Phoebe to have a friend to support her. Do you know her well?'

'I am afraid I do not,' answered Giovanni. 'I have not yet met her. I am …was … Marco's good friend. I had a ticket to come over next week, for the wedding. I am Marco's best man. When

I heard what had happened to him – to them, I thought I should come over still, to escort him home, and make things easier for his Phoebe.'

'Do come through to the sitting room. I'll call her for you.'

Giovanni sat awkwardly on the sofa, waiting to meet his best friend's fiancée. He had been looking forward to the meeting but now – well, nothing had turned out as any of them had expected. When Phoebe walked into the sitting room Giovanni was shocked. The photos that Marco had sent him with the wedding invitation had been of a beautiful young woman. Now Phoebe was tear stained and haggard, with none of the joy and hope he had seen in the pictures. She looked scared and exhausted, and very pregnant. Of course, Giovanni had known they were expecting a child, but hadn't realised that it was due so soon.

Struggling with his own sorrow for the loss of his closest friend, Giovanni began to wish he hadn't come. He didn't feel ready to cope with Phoebe's grief too. He took a deep breath and stood up. It was time to pull himself together. He was an officer in the Polizia di Stato, the Italian Police Force. Surely he was strong enough to comfort an emotional young woman. After all, they were both grieving for the same person. They must have something in common.

Phoebe straightened her shoulders and lifted her chin. This was Marco's best friend, and even now, she still wanted to make a good impression, for Marco's sake.

'Thank you so much for coming,' she said, attempting a smile. 'How did you know where to find me?'

'I received a phone call,' Giovanni answered. 'A lady called Pamela Martindale phoned, to tell me about tomorrow's service. I think she just rang me as a curtesy. She was not expecting me to arrive here, but I had a plane ticket, ready for the wedding so I just changed the dates... It felt appropriate to come here to escort you both.'

'Thank you,' said Phoebe, gratefully. 'I'm so glad you did.'

As Giovanni and Phoebe got to know each other, Saraf, taking care to remain invisible, peered around the door to watch them.

'Now what do we do?' she asked. 'Should we tell him what's been going on?'

'No,' answered Fen, firmly, 'He doesn't know about us, the demon, the blood, any of it and we have to keep it that way, or there'll be hell to pay.'

23

Snig hadn't managed to persuade Glint not to fetch the demons, but he did convince his fellow imp to delay a little … take a bit of time to let his damaged body recover before returning to his demonic masters. After all, just because imps were supposed to obey demons, that didn't mean they had to be slavish about. Snig was discovering that he had a bit of a taste for rebellion. Perhaps it was time the imps stood up for themselves.

This meant that by the time Glint returned to where he'd left Dread and the others, and then led them to Stow, it was almost dawn. Too late to begin their attack on the girl when she was tucked up in bed inside the vicarage, especially with angels standing guard.

Dire suggested that they waited until that evening … but Dread was becoming impatient. He wanted the girl's blood, and he wanted it right away. All the demons were concentrating on that, partly because it stopped them worrying about being trapped in the world in their demon forms, with no obvious way to get back into the Darkness. It was a strange feeling, being unable to get home. Usually they spent their time trying to find a way into the world, to collect soul-lights and return to the Darkness empowered. Now they were anxious about being able to get back there at all.

Dread was raging up and down the vicarage garden, pulling up plants and kicking flower pots over. Every so often, just for variety, he would smash his fist into Glint's face. The imp tried not to squeal, as that only seemed to make the demon even angrier.

'We have to act now,' Dread was saying, not even bothering to keep his voice down. 'All we need to do is get our claws on that girl, rip her apart and drink her blood, and then the angels won't be able to stop us. We'll be powerful enough to do anything we want.'

The other demons finally agreed, but none of them wanted to be the one to go into the vicarage and drag the girl out - not alone, anyway.

'We wait until she comes out, then,' insisted Dire, 'Even if it's full daylight. We just charge, grab her and go for the kill. It'll be over in moments, and we'll be too strong to be defeated. Then we scatter and each of us tries to make our own way back to the Darkness. The angels will have too many targets to follow all of us, and they'll be too busy worrying about letting their charge die.' Since nobody had a better plan, the demons decided to wait.

Snig watched them from up in the branches of a tree, determined to keep out of the way of the demons. The less they noticed him, the better. His perch above the garden gave him an excellent view of the back door, which opened in response to all the noise that Dread had been making, and a childlike angel stepped out.

The imp watched her look out over the garden, then call to somebody inside the house to come and join her. Another angel came to the door, and Snig remembered where he had seen him before - at the caves when the entrance back into the Darkness had been sealed. Two angels to protect one human seemed a bit over the top to Snig but what did he know? He watched as the angels silently circled the garden, looking for whoever had been causing the disturbance. Snig considered warning the demons, but decided against it. Why should he? They were big and ugly enough to look after themselves. Besides, observing a battle might be more fun than taking part or taking sides. He wasn't going to warn the angels about the demons either.

Fen and Saraf moved silently through the garden as the sky began to lighten. It was Saraf who had noticed the sound of someone outside first. Fen was close behind her, and both were expecting trouble. To be honest Fen had been thankful for a day or so of peace while James and Pam had been making all the arrangements for Marco's funeral service, and the repatriation of the young man's body. Now everything was settled, perhaps it would be better to have the showdown with the demon at once. Then they could escort Phoebe to Rome knowing that she was out of immediate danger and the girl would be able to grieve in peace.

They rounded the corner of the shrubbery at the bottom of the garden and froze. They'd been expecting trouble, to be taking on a demon, but not seven of them. That was not something that they had prepared for. Dread they recognised from his attack on Phoebe's flat, and Glint, the imp, they had both seen before, but they had no idea where six other demons had come from. Nor did they think they could fight that many of the creatures at once. Well, they knew they could fight them, they didn't have a choice, but they weren't at all sure they could win.

The demons turned out from their angry cluster and bared their teeth. They were spoiling for a fight, and with the angels so outnumbered perhaps it wouldn't matter if the battle came before they drank the girl's blood or after. Either way the result would be the same. Two dead angels and seven satisfied demons.

Dread charged at Saraf, picking on her as the obviously weaker member of the angelic team. Saraf twisted out of his path, and spun round, holding the cross she wore around her neck in front of her. Dread, beginning another charge, paused for a moment. He remembered how much contact with that had hurt during their last encounter. Suddenly another type of pain struck him as Fen squirted Holy Water into his eyes.

James had filled some plant spray bottles with it the night before when they'd been battling the imps, and Fen had grabbed the one left beside the back door when he and Saraf came out to investigate the noise. Dread was temporarily blinded and began stumbling about, clutching wildly with his claws, hoping to sink them into one of the angels. Instead he caught hold of another of the demons, Drool, and the two began fighting each other.

Another burst of spray had the other demons backing off a

little until they were out of range. Saraf looked at Fen in a panic. Even with two of the demons fighting each other that still left five circling, waiting to attack them, and Fen wasn't sure how much Holy Water was left in the spray bottle. He hated the idea of retreating, but they weren't prepared for an attack on this scale. If they fought on the demons would probably destroy them, and then there'd be nobody to protect Phoebe. Reluctantly, Fen signalled Saraf to go back into the house while he covered their retreat, using the remaining Holy Water to keep the demons back until both angels were safely inside. Up in his tree Snig chuckled. He's rather enjoyed watching that, although there was disappointingly little blood and gore.

Dread had ripped and torn blindly at Drool, the demon he'd grabbed hold of, and had continued with such ferocity that when some sight returned to his burned and blistered eyes, he discovered he'd dismembered him completely. Dread wiped his hands on the grass to rid them of the dead demon's sticky yellow saliva.

Drool's remains were spread around his feet, while Dire and the others watched in fascination. None of them had felt tempted to intervene. After all, one dead demon meant more of the girl's blood for the rest of them. What interested them all was what would happen to the demon's body now it was dead. That might give them a clue about how to get back home. They waited to see if the demon's essence rose from its dead body and dispersed back into the Darkness. That was usually what would happen in a demon was attacked while in the human world. The human body it inhabited might die, but the demon lived on.

Not this time. Dead demon was still dead demon. No essence. No disappearing body parts. No way back into the familiar comfort of the Darkness. Just lots of lumps of demon flesh. Daunt wondered if the stuff was tasty, and reached out to try a little portion. He bit unto a chunk of thigh and then spat it out. Apparently, even demons found demon flesh disgusting. No surprise there.

They kicked the pieces of their dead companion into the bushes, and continued planning their attack on the girl. They'd lost the element of surprise, but they still out-numbered the angels three to one. They would win eventually. Looking down on them through the branches Snig noticed that Glint was cowering behind an apple tree, hoping that they wouldn't notice him, and the other demons were giving Dread a wide berth. Not that demons were ever loyal to each other, but they certainly weren't going to trust one that had just killed one of their own.

24

Faced with a situation that was far more menacing than the angels had at first thought, they held a council of war in the kitchen. It was just as well that Giovanni had booked himself into a guest house in the town, as trying to keep things secret in such a crisis would have been extremely difficult. Phoebe was asleep, and they decided to leave her that way. She needed some rest, and they all wanted her to be able to concentrate on the service for Marco without being distracted by just how bad the situation was.

Banking on the fact that the demons might take a little time to regroup, Fen sent Saraf to the High Council with a request for help, while James phoned Pam and asked her to ring around everyone in the church prayer chain. Not that they could be told precisely what they were praying for, just that the memorial service that morning, and the girl who'd lost her fiancée, needed a lot of prayer cover, and could anyone who was free please come to the service to lend their support.

James went to the church to prepare, making sure that he blessed the water he added to the font, in case more Holy Water was needed, and reading aloud any of the bible verses he knew to be helpful against anything from the Darkness, just to refresh his memory. He unlocked the north door, the one flanked by the yew trees, in case a second exit was needed. It was only used occasionally, such as when the church was packed for events like the Christmas tree festival, and the key could be awkward to turn in the lock. He checked that the large metal cross was in its usual place on the alter, should it be needed, and spent some time in prayer. That was as ready as he could get. He was grateful that the service was arranged for that morning, and would be followed by Phoebe and Giovanni leaving immediately to accompany Marco's coffin to Rome. He couldn't believe how quickly he had managed to arrange for the body to be repatriated. It involved the kind of bureaucracy that normally took weeks to cut through. He put it down to prayers being answered and hoped that the rest of the day would go as smoothly.

By mid-day people were arriving at the church. Fen had warned Phoebe to speak to anyone she needed to before the service as she'd have to leave immediately afterwards to escort the coffin to the airport and on to Rome. He didn't tell her quite why she'd need to make such a speedy exit. Time enough for that later.

Giovanni, followed by Fen, walked with Phoebe to the church, making their way in through the main South doors, which were flung open to welcome both the congregation and the coffin. In front of Phoebe, but unseen by anybody, walked Celeste and Able – a show of strength to deter the demons, for a while at least. Fen found the presence of two such powerful angels reassuring. They all knew that there weren't enough angels to give anyone that level of protection for long, but having them there, even briefly, helped

As they entered the church Phoebe could feel a great sense of peace, like a comforting blanket wrapping itself around her. It was created by the prayers of many of the people in the church, and it seemed to lift some of the weight of misery off her shoulders for a while, enabling her to concentrate on the words James was speaking. She even managed not to crumble when Marco's coffin was carried into the church. Giovanni supported her on one side, and Fen, invisible, on the other. Saraf, also unseen, was standing beside the alter, alongside James, while Pam moved over to sit behind the girl, armed with a glass of water and a packet of tissues. Pam was always practical, whatever the situation.

Before the service began James invited those who'd come to remember Marco to take a few minutes to talk to Phoebe, explaining that she wouldn't be able to stay after the service. As most of the friends who had come weren't really sure what to say in such a situation, this didn't take long, although she appreciated their hugs and their support.

Phoebe was surprised and touched to see the Head of the Art department, from their course. He took her aside and encouraged her to keep painting, when she was ready.

'The world has lost Marco's talent,' he said, 'it shouldn't lose yours too. Besides painting can be a good way of remembering, and of dealing with grief.'

'Thank you,' Phoebe said.

The service began, although none of those inside could see that there were four angels standing guard throughout it. Nor were they aware of the six demons prowling around the churchyard. Despite their blustering about attacking Phoebe as soon as she came out of the vicarage, the presence of the additional angels, and the bright sunlight, and crowded streets had deterred them, and they had missed their chance.

Now they were attempting to come up with a new plan. They expected Phoebe to follow the coffin out of the main doors of the church as the funeral service finished. That would be their chance to grab her

Dread was still unnerving the other demons. He seemed to be in a permanent rage now, since things weren't going to plan, which made him unpredictable. His wild emotions had also drawn the remaining Lesser Invisibles to the demons. There were only three imps that James and Fen, and Pam's unfortunate driving accident, had missed, but for once they were finding watching demons much more entertaining than winding up humans.

Inside the church James was leading the service, trying to make it as personal as he could about someone he had never met. He had drawn on details he'd picked up talking to Phoebe and to Giovanni, about what Marco was like, and to her surprise Phoebe really did find the words he spoke comforting. She stood up to say a few words herself, but struggled to get them out without crying. However, she managed it, and walked back to her seat with her head held high, though she was glad to accept some tissues and a sip of water from Pam afterwards. Giovanni spoke briefly too, and James invited any others amongst Marco's friends to say a few words if they wanted to. It ended up feeling more like a celebration of Marco's life than Phoebe had expected, and she was glad that James had arranged it.

As the service drew to a close, Fen opened the church doors a crack, and saw the demons gathered at the front. He signalled to Saraf, who carefully opened the North door a little, ready to usher Phoebe out that way. The funeral directors carried the coffin out of the main doors and towards the hearse, but as she followed them Phoebe felt a tug on her arm, pulling her towards the other door. Knowing better than to argue by now, Phoebe hurried to the north door, while James and Giovanni followed the coffin. If anyone wondered why James had taken the large metal alter cross with him, they were too polite to ask.

Eager to detract the rest of the congregation, Pam gathered everyone around the urn at the back of the church, explaining that Phoebe had to hurry away but everybody else was invited to stay for refreshments. A delicious array of cakes and biscuits was uncovered, Pam's friend Ivy having outdone herself, and the whole congregation remained in the church for tea, and to reminisce about Marco, as Pam had hoped. Jean, who had done the flowers for the funeral, received lots of well-deserved compliments about them as she helped serve the teas and coffees. All in all, everything was rather pleasant, inside the church - as pleasant as a funeral can be, anyway.

'There's a bit of a draft today,' said Pam, hurrying over to close the main doors, so that nobody could see what was going on outside, where things were rather less jolly.

James had thrust a puzzled Giovanni into the funeral car on the street that ran beside the churchyard, while the coffin was being placed in the hearse. Thankfully the high churchyard wall hid what was now going on outside the church, where the demons were battling it out with the angels.

'Where is Phoebe?' Giovanni asked James. 'She did not follow us out?'

'She used the other door,' said James, making it up on the spot. 'It's a tradition here. Widows and such, always leave a funeral by the north door to greet the yew trees … for luck.' He ground to a halt as Giovanni looked at him as if he'd gone mad. James briefly wondered if perhaps he had.

'I'll go and get her,' said the vicar, hurrying away. He ran up the steps into the churchyard to see Fen, Celeste and Able fighting with the demons. Strengthened by prayer and prepared for the attack this time the angels were fighting back with Holy Water, holy words and brute force.

Although the angels were outnumbered, they were putting up a good fight, and distracting the demons. In this they were both hindered and assisted by the remaining imps, drawn to the fight by Dread's raging emotions. These creatures were jumping in and out of the melee, attacking whoever was nearest, just for fun. To James it looked as if the imps were doing more damage to the demons than the angels. Every so often some Holy Water would splash onto an imp, which would vanish back into the Darkness.

Thumping a demon on the head with the metal cross on his way past, James ran around to the back of the church where Phoebe was standing beside Saraf, in the archway formed by the two old yew trees. None of them noticed Snig and Glint, each tucked behind one of the tree trunks, observing what was going on.

'Do you think we ought to call out?' asked Glint, in a whisper. 'Tell the demons that the girl is back here.'

'Probably,' answered Snig, softly. 'Let's give it couple of minutes though, eh?'

With the young angel leading the way and the vicar running behind wielding the cross like a weapon, Phoebe sprinted around the church and down the steps onto the street, practically falling into the funeral car. Deciding that pregnancy and running didn't mix, Phoebe struggled to get her breath back.

Leaning out of the car she turned to James and gave him a clumsy hug.

'Thank you, for everything … and thank Pam for me too. I'm sorry I didn't get a chance to say goodbye to her.'

'She'll understand' replied James. 'And you're welcome. Good luck with everything. And God Bless you. You'll be in my prayers.'

'We'll need them,' said Phoebe, solemnly. 'Oh, what about our luggage?'

'It's in the boot,' James smiled. 'I had the driver collect it before the funeral, yours and Giovanni's. Now go.' He slammed the door shut and shouted to the driver to get going, which he did, following the hearse through the busy market square.

James walked back into the churchyard and nodded, at which point Saraf and Fen knew that Phoebe had set off safely on her journey. They drew back from the fight, although Saraf was a little disappointed as she'd only just got started. One of the demons was still on the ground, though whether dead or unconscious James couldn't tell. The vicar thought it might have been the one he thumped with the cross, but he wasn't quite sure.

The demons suddenly realised that Phoebe had vanished. Their desire to find her being greater than their enthusiasm for the fight, they too stepped back, and began to look around for their prey. Dire kicked the demon who was on the ground, but it didn't move. Another one gone. As the angels closed in on them again, the demons drew back, hurrying round to the back of the churchyard, out of sight.

'What am I meant to do with that?' asked James, alarmed, as he nudged the demon body lying dead on the ground. 'I can hardly call the police, or an undertaker and the congregation will start coming out soon.'

'Leave it to us,' said Celeste crisply. 'And thank you, James.'

'Yes, thank you,' added Fen. 'For all your help. Now we'd ...' he glanced at Celeste, 'I mean I'd better catch up with Phoebe.'

'There's another dead demon in James's garden,' Saraf whispered to Celeste, then she reached up to give James a parting hug, and lifted up into the air.

Making sure to adjust their wingbeats to avoid being seen, the two angels headed in the direction the funeral car had taken.

Celeste and her fellow angel dragged the demon's corpse out of sight behind some bushes to dispose of later, and James re-entered the church, trying to look as if he was having a perfectly normal day.

25

Since the funeral car was following the hearse to the airport at a moderate speed, it didn't take too long for Fen and Saraf to catch up with it. Then they flew above it until the vehicles reached the end of their journey. They watched solemnly as the coffin was transferred into the hold of the plane, and then Phoebe and Giovanni boarded the flight with the other passengers. The angels chose to travel in the hold with the coffin. The cold didn't bother them, and it meant they wouldn't have to concentrate of remaining invisible, they could relax and build their strength up after the fight. They settled into a comfortable silence, as did Phoebe and Giovanni in their seats above, both too tired, emotionally at least, to try and carry on a conversation.

The demons, however, were not so peaceful. Dread was shouting for Glint, who reluctantly climbed down from his cosy spot behind the trunk of the yew tree. He noticed that Snig had slipped away, and wished he'd had the sense to do the same thing before the demons had come around to the back of the church.

Now the imp was cowering before his master. He had a nasty feeling that he knew what the next order would be.

'Find her,' demanded Dread, just as Glint had feared. 'Find her or I'll rip you apart.'

'I can't,' groaned the imp. 'I can't sense her any more. The effect of her blood has worn off.' The demons could see the creature was telling the truth, he no longer looked special, he had returned to being just an ordinary, ugly, little imp.

As Glint had expected Dread and the other demons took the news badly, and promptly took their frustration out on him. Soon he was a bleeding heap on the ground, beaten, bitten and kicked.

Since he was of no further use to the demons, they left him there to die, as they hurried away to find some cover until it was dark. If they couldn't use the imp to lead them to the girl, they'd have to try more ordinary methods.

Once he was certain they'd gone, Glint dug his claws into the grass and dragged himself back to the shelter of the yew trees, hoping to die in peace.

Snig had a better idea. He had returned to the churchyard at dusk, having spent a pleasant afternoon charging through the charity shops like a whirlwind, scattering their stock across the floor and terrifying the volunteers who worked in them. He spotted his fellow imp unconscious beside the trees, and tried to drag him away, but he wasn't strong enough to lift him ... not alone. He sat down to consider what to do next.

Snig had caused as much mischief as he could in the town, now he was working alone, and he wasn't supposed to cause humans any lasting harm so he was running out of ideas about what to try next. The truth was, he was getting bored and decided it was time to go back to the Darkness, but this time he really felt he had to try and take Glint with him, to rescue him from the demons, although his motives had more to do with getting one over on those tyrannical creatures, rather than out of kindness for another imp. Kindness was weakness after all, and the only way to survive in the Darkness was to be as strong as possible.

He supposed there was Holy Water in the church, but he really couldn't face coming into contact with the agony that it caused again. Not so soon, anyway. Creeping round to the front of the church confirmed his suspicion that all the angels had departed, so he could only think of one other way to get home: he needed to find someone to pray at him – not a pleasant process but he had to try. He made his way towards the vicarage, wondering whether he was making a terrible mistake.

James and Pam were sitting down with much needed cups of coffee, relieved the bizarre stresses of that particular funeral service were over.

'I think it passed off rather well,' said Pam. 'All things considered.'

'Are you sure nobody at the service saw anything strange?' asked James, popping a slice of left-over cake onto his plate.

'Of course not, thanks to Ivy's baking,' replied Pam. 'Everyone was so busy munching on cakes and chatting about how much they were going to miss Marco, and how tragic it all was for Phoebe and the baby, that nobody ventured out of the church until it was all over. I am rather glad our part in all this is done.'

'Until the next time Celeste comes calling for our help,' James pointed out. 'I know what you mean though, it has been rather intense. I'd be more than happy if our services weren't required for several months.'

'Same here,' agreed Pam. 'At least it's over for us, but what about poor Phoebe? Whatever those creatures want her for, I get the impression that it's never going to be over.'

There was a scraping sound against the window, which was a little odd, as there wasn't any breeze to set the branches of the bushes dancing against it. James went and looked through the glass but he couldn't see anything. Then there was another tentative scraping sound, this time coming from the back door. James opened it and looked out, but didn't see anyone. Suddenly he felt a pain in his foot. He looked down to see an imp hitting his shoe with a half brick he kept outside the door to use as a doorstop, to get his attention.

'Owwww!' said James, reaching for the spray bottle of Holy Water.

'No,' cried Snig. 'Not that stuff, it hurts. Wait, I need your help. Two of us do. Follow.'

Snig began to scuttle away, leaving a confused James on the doorstep. He hadn't even known that imps could talk. Dealing with an influx of them had always felt more like pest control, to be honest. He called for Pam to come with him, and they set off after Snig.

They soon found themselves at the north door of the church where Snig had led them, looking at another imp, this one badly injured.

'We need help,' said Snig awkwardly. 'To get home. Not Holy Water ... it burns ... Glint's too sick. Not a kick. Pray us back into the Darkness.'

Pam and James stared at each other, flummoxed. This was not a situation they'd ever expected to find themselves in.

'All right,' agreed James, 'But I'd like to know who did this to him. Was it one of the angels?'

'Course not,' said Snig defiantly. 'They just send us home. Only demons try to kill us.'

James and Pamela joined together in prayer. Anyone passing would have been puzzled to see the young vicar and an older lady praying beside the yew tree, with two strange little creatures huddled at their feet. They would have been even more confused when each of the creatures gave a yelp and vanished from sight. Thankfully nobody had been passing, and the imps were driven back into the darkness unobserved.

When it was finished Pam looked at James and remarked, 'I think I need a cup of tea.'

'I think I need something stronger than that,' said James with a grin. 'Fancy a quick drink in The Queen's Head?'

'Why not,' replied Pam, 'The sun is well and truly over the yard arm, and in this case, I think we've earned a drink.'

The mis-matched pair made their way out of the churchyard and across the market square to the atmospheric old pub.

26

The demons had to wait until it was fully dark before putting their new plan into action. Given that Glint could no longer help them track the girl, they'd have to discover where she'd gone using more ordinary skills. There were two funeral directors in Stow, so the remaining five demons split into two groups; each picked a business to break into.

It was the group that Dire was leading that discovered the paperwork about that day's funeral. He read the documents in horror, before re-joining the rest of the demons and telling them the bad news.

'Rome?' Dread was beside himself. 'The girl can't have gone to Rome. We can't follow her there.'

'We could try,' suggested one of the demons. Dread turned on him, furious.

'And just how exactly do you suggest we 'try'?' He demanded. 'Hitch a lift to another country, looking like THIS?'

'It must be possible,' said Dire, calmly, pacing up and down as he tried to think. 'We have two choices. We try to follow the girl, or we wait until she comes back.'

'Who knows how long that will be,' shouted Dread. 'We can't just stay here twiddling our claws forever.'

'Rome it is, then,' replied Dire, snidely. 'But don't get too excited. First, we have to figure out a way to get there, and that's going to take some time.'

By the time they landed at Rome's Fiumicino Airport Phoebe felt as if the day had stretched out for an eternity. The scene in the churchyard, of a large group of angels and demons battling it out, had been terrifying, once she'd had time to think about it. For a start, it had appeared to her that the demons were winning. There were certainly more of them. Also, it made her realise what she was up against. Not just one demon but several, and they were all after her blood. She hoped that Fen and Saraf were somewhere nearby. Now she had a better understanding of the situation, she realised just how much she needed their protection. Strangely, she felt as if she needed their company too. She couldn't talk to Giovanni about what was going on, and she wouldn't be able to discuss it with Marco's Nonna Battista either.

Once the plane touched down Phoebe realised how useful it was having Giovanni with her. He took over the arrangements for having the coffin delivered to the church Nonna Battista had chosen, and since she didn't speak much Italian, she was glad that he was there to go through all the documents that proved things she didn't even want to think about.... that the body had been correctly embalmed, the wooden coffin was lined with lead and that the Consular Seals, that had been attached before the body had been driven to the church in Stow, were in place and hadn't been tampered with.

After what seemed like endless conversations, it was done. Marco's coffin was driven away, and Giovanni fetched his car from the airport carpark, helped Phoebe into it and drove her and her luggage to the outskirts of Rome, to Nonna Battista's house.

The old lady's home was surprisingly large and rambling. It was set back from the road, its privacy protected by a high stone wall, and Giovanni turned his car into the drive and parked. He got out of the car and came around to Phoebe's side to open her door and help her out. The gesture was so like Marco's that it was all she could do not to cry.

She looked up at the house, which seemed to have to lights on in every room, making it look warm and welcoming in the dusk. The air outside was warm too. For some reason that took Phoebe by surprise, though it shouldn't have done. Warm air in Rome in summer was hardly unexpected. Perhaps it was because she was there for all the wrong reasons. If they'd come on their honeymoon, she and Marco, they would have been planning the trip, monitoring the weather forecast, deciding they didn't need to pack jumpers. Instead Phoebe braced herself and walked towards the front door, preparing to meet Marco's grandmother for the first time. She hoped that the old lady would like her.

Nonna Battista opened the door and gathered Phoebe up in an enormous hug.

'*Benvenuto*,' she said. 'Come in, come in, both of you. *Grazie*, Giovanni, for bringing Phoebe to me.'

'*Prego*,' the young man replied. 'I'm always happy to help, Nonna. Now I shall leave you two to get acquainted.'

'No, you must come in and join us for dinner,' the old lady insisted.

Phoebe was glad when he agreed. Although she didn't know him well, she didn't know Marco's grandmother at all, and having Giovanni at this difficult meeting helped somehow.

She appreciated them both speaking in English for her benefit. She'd picked up a little Italian from Marco, but not enough to understand a fast-moving discussion.

The meal was delicious but none of them were terribly hungry, and the conversation between them was interspersed with silences as they all struggled to deal with Marco's death. In one of the pauses Phoebe turned to Giovanni.

'Why is your English accent so much better than Marco's was?' she asked. 'After all, he lived there for three years.'

'I was sent to school there,' Giovanni replied. 'My parents were in the diplomatic core so they moved around a lot. I started my secondary education here. That's how Marco and I became friends. But when my parents were posted to India, they thought boarding school was the best option for me. They chose an English one. They thought it would be good for my career if I learned to speak English properly.'

'In the police?' questioned Phoebe.

Nonna laughed ''e choose de police force, but his parents …

dey wanted 'im to be a diplomat, like dem. *Ambassadore* Giovanni ... it has a good sound, yes?'

'Not to me,' said Giovanni, smiling. 'I'm happy to make my own decisions ... just as Marco made his.'

'I never stopped him,' stated Nonna Battista, proudly. 'Marco, 'e wanted to be an artist, I say good boy, off you go!'

'She says that now,' chuckled Giovanni, 'But at the time, she was all ... an artist? You'll never make any money. You'll starve, Marco, you'll starve.' Nonna joined in with the laughter.

'You know what 'e say to me?' she asked Phoebe. ''e say, "all de best artists starve, and I'll be one of de best".' This was so typical of Marco's confidence and enthusiasm that they all started laughing, and Phoebe began to relax for the first time since her arrival in Rome; but she noticed that Marco's grandmother quickly struggled for breath, and the old lady's hands were shaking as they cleared the table together.

Phoebe suggested that it was time for bed, but Nonna picked a coat up from a hook by the front door,

'Not for me. Not tonight. Tonight, I go to de church for de vigil. I say de prayers for de dead and sit with my *nipote* ... my grandson.'

Phoebe struggled to her feet, saying 'Then I'll come with you.'

'Not tonight, *figlia,* you must rest, you and de *bambino.* Tomorrow we 'ave de funeral mass, and we bury my boy. You need to be strong for dat.'

Giovanni drove the old lady to the church, and stayed with her through the night, while Phoebe lay down to rest. It was the first time she'd been alone for hours. She needed to sleep, but before she could, she had to ask some questions. She got up and opened the window of the bedroom she'd been given and called out softly.

'Fen, Saraf, are you there?'

The angels appeared in the shadows below her, then fluttered up and into the room. It was a relief to know that they had travelled with her to Rome, and that she and her baby still had some protection.

'Did anyone get hurt?' she asked. 'I saw a fight going on.'

'Well, there's one less demon to worry about,' replied Fen.

'Will they be able to follow me here? Am I safe now?'

'For the moment,' Fen replied. 'If they can work out where you've gone, they will come after you, but you should be safe for a while at least.'

'Thank you,' said Phoebe. 'But I still don't understand what's going on. Why they want my blood, particularly.'

'We can't tell you,' grinned Saraf. 'It'll only make things worse.'

Given how bad things were already, Phoebe decided she was too tired to push for any more information. The day had been long, tiring and emotional, and tomorrow was likely to be just as tough. She settled down to sleep, exhausted.

27

The next day passed in a blur for Phoebe. Another funeral service, this one in Italian, with lots of people she didn't know crowding round her and Nonna. She was glad to feel the baby kicking inside her at one point during the service. Not only did it comfort her to know the baby was all right, but it reminded her that Marco had left something of himself in the world, and Phoebe was determined to make a happy life for the child, and tell it all about its father when it was old enough.

After the mass the coffin was carried out into the quiet graveyard, and lowered into the ground in the family plot. It seemed Nonna Battista's family did things in style, and Phoebe thought Marco would have appreciated the statues all around, marking the graves. He had loved anything gothic, and the stone angels seemed particularly appropriate. Out of the corner of her eye she saw Saraf, completely visible and standing absolutely still, pretending to be a statue herself, and she couldn't help smiling for a moment, before the sight of Marco's coffin being covered with earth wiped the smile away.

The burial was followed by the wake. More strangers and conversations she couldn't follow. Clutching a glass of juice and nibbling at buffet food she couldn't really bring herself to eat much of. Then it was over.

The day after that both she and Nonna Battista rested, too exhausted, in every way, to do more than shuffle around the house, and chat occasionally about Marco, the baby, and Phoebe's plans for the future. Phoebe tried to sound positive but she couldn't really think beyond being about to give birth, and being chased by demons.

Nonna Battista appeared much frailer than she had when Phoebe had arrived, and Phoebe realised that the old lady had used up much of her strength to get through the vigil and the funeral, and to try and make Phoebe feel welcome and cared for. Now the strain was beginning to show.

Fen and Saraf were outside in the garden. They couldn't risk entering the house, in case Nonna Battista caught a glimpse of them, but for the moment they were content to keep watch from where they were. Saraf was sniffing at some of the bright blooms in the garden.

'I think I've been here before,' she announced. 'Italy, I mean. I remember the smell of flowers like these, and the warmth of the air.'

'Who were you watching over then?' asked Fen, still curious about why Saraf didn't seem to have been given anyone to protect for ages. Her face blanked and she rapidly changed the subject.

'I can't remember … probably nobody. Nonna Battista's soul-light is pretty, isn't it?'

'You know I can't see anyone's except Phoebe's,' he sighed, wishing she hadn't avoided answering his question. 'All right, what colour is it then?' he said, to humour her.

'It's almost white … very pure. That's a good sign, isn't it? But it's getting pale too. Almost see through.'

'That's not so good,' Fen commented, wearily, suspecting it meant the old lady's health was declining.

'No,' agreed Saraf. 'It's sad.' She pulled the head off a flower, restlessly. 'When do you think the demons will get here?'

'I've no idea,' replied Fen, frustrated. 'We need to stay alert. They might not be far behind us.'

They weren't. Once they'd found the address, the demons had made their way to a ferry port. They were afraid they'd be too visible to get away with crossing the tarmac to get into the hold of a plane, even in the dark. Instead they'd managed to climb into the back of a delivery lorry, and eventually, after changing vehicles a couple of times, they'd reached Portsmouth.

After an unpleasant trip hiding beneath the freight lorries on the car deck they landed in France. It had taken them almost twenty-four hours already, and they still had to make their way to Rome.

Some of the demons were starting to protest that it wasn't worth the journey. At least two of them would have turned back if they'd had any way to slip into the Darkness. As it was, they continued the expedition reluctantly, in the hope that something would turn up to get them back home, preferably with Phoebe's blood in their veins.

The following day Giovanni arrived on the doorstep early in the morning and announced that he was going to take Phoebe out for the day. She tried to protest that she wasn't in the right frame of mind for sight-seeing, but he insisted.

'Marco wanted to show you his country, to share it with you' said Giovanni firmly. 'Soon you will return to England, the baby will come, and who knows when you will have this chance again. Surely you are a little curious?'

'Go with 'im,' said Nonna Battista. 'It is good to be distracted for a while, Marco would be 'appy for dis.'

'Where are we going?' Phoebe asked.

'Anywhere Marco would have taken you,' grinned Giovanni, 'Come on.'

'Wait a minute,' she said. 'He made a list, it's in my room. I'll go and fetch it.'

She hurried up the stairs and hunted in her bag for Marco's list. She came across her camera at the bottom of her bag, and hesitated. Taking a camera with her seemed such a holidayish thing to do … but she might regret it if she didn't. Next to the camera was Marco's mobile. They only had the one between them and had never used it much, since the landline at the flat was so much cheaper. She noticed there were some text messages waiting to be read, but she couldn't face it. She flung the phone on the bed, and took Marco's list and the camera downstairs.

'Let me see what he was planning,' said Giovanni, taking the piece of paper. 'Charming' he laughed, 'As well as the obvious places like the Coliseum and St Peter's Basilica, he was planning to drag you to the Catacombs and the Caputchin Crypt.'

Nonna tutted fondly. 'Dat boy. 'e 'ad a passion for bones. So unsuitable for a day out with a young lady.'

'Let's do it. Show me Rome ... even the grisly bits. It's what Marco would have wanted.'

Nonna Battista hurried them out of the door, warning Giovanni not to let Phoebe get too exhausted. 'De girl is pregnant, don't forget,' she called after them.

As if anyone could forget, thought Phoebe, given the size of the bump she was carrying round with her.

Giovanni began their day out with what he claimed would he a whistle-stop tour of Rome, but given the crowded state of the roads the journey wasn't as hair raising as Phoebe had feared. They drove past the Vatican and St Peter's Basilica, with Giovanni looking for somewhere to park, but when Phoebe saw the number of people queuing to go in, she crossed that off her list.

'Not when I'm this pregnant,' she said to Giovanni with a grin. 'We'd have to stand in line for hours. It's very kind of you to show me around,' she added, 'but are you sure you have time for this?'

'I had booked this week as leave anyway,' he answered, not looking at her. Of course, he had been coming to England for the wedding, which would have been tomorrow.

Neither of them wanted to refer to what they'd lost, so in order to distract them, Giovanni drove Phoebe around Rome pointing out some of the sights.

'Now you need to get closer to some of these beautiful places,' said Giovanni. 'Where would you like to start?'

Phoebe glanced down at the list she was holding in her hand. 'How about the Catacombs?' she said. 'Marco would have liked that.'

Giovanni explained that there were several of these

underground cemeteries and he drove her to one just outside of the town. This was called the Catacombe di Domitilla. Everyone else was arriving in groups, but Giovanni had a friend who worked at the site as a guide, which made it possible to go in without being part of a tour.

Although it was warm outside, the narrow tunnels were chilly, and Giovanni's friend explained that they were in the oldest burial tunnels in the world.

'They were built in the second century because Rome was so short of land that there was nowhere left to put people's remains, and it was against the law to bury people inside the city. Originally the tunnels would have been lined with human bones, but now there are no longer any bones or skulls remaining in the alcoves that line the tunnel walls.'

The place was wonderfully atmospheric, and there were some beautiful frescos, so Phoebe could see why Marco had wanted to take her there.

Their second stop was more of a challenge. Phoebe had asked Giovanni about the Capuchin Crypt which was the next place on Marco's list.

'Is it to do with monkeys?' she asked, puzzled.

'Nothing like that at all.' Giovanni chuckled, 'It's connected with the Capuchin Monks but I don't know if you're ready to visit it.'

'Why?' asked Phoebe.

'There are bones,' he replied, 'Lots of bones. It might be too soon.'

'It might be my only chance,' countered Phoebe. 'Come on, if Marco liked the place, I might too.'

'Or you might not,' said Giovanni, worried, as he parked up near the museum that housed the crypt.

28

As Giovanni led Phoebe through the museum, she paused to look at a beautiful picture of St Francis painted by Caravaggio. The Saint was kneeling, looking reverently at a skull that he was holding in his hands. The expression on his face and the muted colours of his robe were so realistic, that Phoebe would usually have stared at it for hours, soaking up the details and committing it to memory, but Giovanni was tugging at her arm, eager to lead her down into the crypt.

Phoebe couldn't believe her eyes when they reached it. It was made up of several tiny chapels beneath the church, and she was stunned to see that these were lined and decorated with the bones and skeletons of hundreds of dead monks. She found the bones were making far more of an impact on her than the beautiful painting she'd been looking at a few minutes before.

Giovanni explained that the displays weren't meant to be macabre, but were supposed to act as a reminder of how brief life is and that we all die eventually. Given the circumstances neither of them felt they needed much reminding about that, but Phoebe was surprised to find the displays strangely beautiful. Apparently, they had started when the monks had moved the remains of their predecessors to this new site, and had to work out what to do with so many disarticulated bones. After that it became an honour for monks of the order to join the bony symbols on the walls after their death.

While some of the bones were arranged in decorative stacks against the walls of the chapels, others were fixed onto the walls and ceilings to form patterns. Some were adapted to form chandeliers, others were in the shape of clocks, or hour glasses with wings, formed by shoulder blades, to remind visitors of how fast time flew. There were even a few whole skeletons, still dressed in monk's robes, with dry skin stretched across their skulls and sightless eyes staring across the room, and a figure holding a scythe and scales ... symbols of death, and judgement. Nearby a placard read:

WHAT YOU ARE NOW WE USED TO BE;
WHAT WE ARE NOW YOU WILL BE

Phoebe expected to find it all creepy, most of the visitors to the crypt seemed to. Instead she was fascinated. She could see why these images had appealed to Marco, and she had a sudden urge to paint them, though they were not her usual subject matter at all.

Fen and Saraf had followed them around the display, keeping themselves invisible. Fen was more interested in Phoebe's reaction to the bones than in the displays themselves but it was Saraf who was really revolted.

'Those are disgusting,' she announced. 'They ought to be properly buried, in Holy ground.'

'This is Holy ground,' Fen pointed out. 'These are all chapels. That's why visitors aren't allowed to take pictures.'

'Who'd want to,' complained Saraf. 'This place is horrible.'

Phoebe felt differently. Respecting the instruction not to take photos, she was choosing postcards in the gift shop, trying to pick as many different images as possible, to inspire her when she next had a chance to paint. When she got to the counter, she realised she had no Euros and had to borrow some off Giovanni. He wasn't sure if he'd done the right thing in bringing her to this particular museum, but Phoebe insisted that helped her to feel closer to Marco, to understand his interest in the macabre, and his desire to paint it.

Once they had walked back to the car Giovanni could see that the girl was shattered, and drove her back to Nonna Battista's house, promising to take her out again the next day.

By the time they arrived at Nonna Battista's home, the demons had just reached the house, and were lurking in the bushes near the gates onto the drive.

'I'll collect you tomorrow morning,' Giovanni said. 'We'll go to the Coliseum, and to another of Marco's less obvious suggestions, the Basilica of St Clemente.' Giovanni then explained that this was built on top of ancient ruins, set on top of an even older structure.

'Wrap up warmly,' Giovanni instructed, just before he drove away. 'It can be cold and dark down there.'

'Cold and dark,' muttered Dread from his hiding place. 'The perfect spot for an attack.'

'And the ideal place to hide,' added Dire, grimacing at the other demons. 'We could go there now, and set up an ambush. That way those angels won't be expecting us.'

Reluctant as he was to agree with another demon, Dread could see the logic of the suggestion. The creatures slipped quietly away, heading into the centre of Rome.

Fen eventually managed to drag Saraf away from the bone crypt and they flew back to Nonna Battista's house. Fen searched the grounds anxiously, concerned that the demons could turn up at any moment. It never occurred to him that they'd already been ... and gone.

Marco's grandmother had sent Phoebe upstairs to rest for a while, worried about how tired she looked when she got in, but the girl couldn't settle. She got out a sketchbook and started to doodle.

She couldn't get the images from the crypt out of her mind. For the first time she could see why Marco had found death and decay so appealing as source material for his art. It suited her present mood far more than her usual landscapes and bright colours. And in the light of what she'd been learning about the presence of demons, as well as angels in the world, death seemed different somehow. Less final, perhaps, or scarier, depending on how you looked at it. Glancing down at what she'd drawn she was surprised to see it was actually rather good. There was an energy to it she hadn't expected, and she realised she'd woven the glimpses she'd had of the demons into the sketches of the skeletons and bone patterns from the crypt.

She sketched some of the frescos from the catacombs as well, and found the early Christian art an interesting contrast to the darker images she'd been drawing. She wondered if she could find a way to blend them together and it crossed her mind that Marco would have approved. Then she realised that this was the first time since the accident that she'd managed to think of him in a positive way ... not just about his death, and her loss, but about Marco the person. Marco the artist.

Phoebe was thankful to have the time to do that, before the chaos started again, and the demons caught up with her. She was grateful to Fen and Saraf too, for their protection which gave her this breathing space, and a chance to grieve normally.

She wandered down to have dinner with Nonna Battista, unaware that this would be her last evening of peace and safety for a very long time.

29

Sharing their evening meal, Phoebe found she could talk more naturally to Nonna Battista than she'd been able too when she first arrived in Rome. She felt she was getting to know the old lady a little, and to like her a lot. She was looking forward to her baby having Nonna as a great grandmother, although she didn't know how often she'd be able to afford to bring the child to visit.

'Do not fret about such dings,' said Marco's grandmother. 'When de time is right, I will buy tickets. Marco was my only grandchild. On who else shall I spend money?'

'Are you sure you don't mind me going off with Giovanni again tomorrow?' Phoebe asked. 'It seems rude to stay with you, but be out all day,'

'My Marco, 'e would be happy for dis, 'e wanted you to see 'is city, and if 'e can't show it to you, 'e would be glad Giovanni do it for 'im. Also, I 'ave things I must do tomorrow … appointments. Dull matters. Better you see some more of de city. Just don't wear out yourself. It will not be long now until de *bambini* arrives. You are tired still. You should go up now, get some sleep. Dat way you will be ready for de morning.'

'After tomorrow, I should start planning to go back to England,' said Phoebe, standing up to go up to bed. 'I can't stay here much longer.'

'You are welcome to stay as long as you choose,' Nonna smiled at her, 'But if you want to go home before de *bambino* comes den, yes, you must travel soon.'

'Before I do, I need to take a picture of you,' said Phoebe, getting her camera out of her bag. 'That way I'll have something I can show to the baby, before we come to visit.'

Phoebe took a couple of snaps of Nonna Battista, and then, remembering the timer on the camera, she set up a picture of the two of them together, and just managed to reach the old lady's side before the shutter clicked.

'I think I needed to allow myself more time to get back to you,' laughed Phoebe. 'Being pregnant is slowing me down.' She kissed Nonna Battista on the cheek and went upstairs to bed. When she reached her room, she found Fen and Saraf waiting for her. They'd been giving her some space for a few days, and she appreciated it, but they all knew the situation couldn't last.

'I'm sorry, Phoebe,' said Fen, 'But we need to start making plans.'

The girl nodded, sadly. 'I know. It's been so peaceful, staying here with Marco's grandmother. Having time to get used to Marco being gone,' she forced herself to say it, 'Being dead.'

'But it can't go on for ever' Saraf chipped in. 'The demons will track you down.'

Phoebe had picked up her sketch pad and was doodling again, to try and help herself think. She found she was creating images of Fen, and of Saraf, and was rather pleased with how they turned out.

'I know that,' Phoebe agreed, 'I can't stay here much longer. I need to get back home, before the baby comes. It won't be long now.' She put her hand on the bump which was wriggling again, 'But I don't even know where home is anymore. Before, it was anywhere Marco and I could be together, but now ...'

Saraf reached out and put her hand on Phoebe's belly, and the baby leapt in response.

'Feel it, Fen,' the younger angel insisted, grinning in delight. Fen looked embarrassed, but Phoebe gave him an encouraging smile so he too leant forward to touch the bump. Again, the baby kicked wildly, joyfully, taking Phoebe's breath away. She smiled at her two protectors, and they smiled back.

Behind his smile, however, Fen was worried, suddenly aware that the baby too, was a living breathing person, almost ready to enter the world, and also in need of his protection. Presumably, once the child was born, he would be its guardian too … unless that was why the High Council had allowed Saraf to stay with him. Maybe she'd be given the baby to protect. Surely, she was due to be put in charge of somebody soon, and the child would need protecting: it too would have angel blood in its veins.

Phoebe put down her sketch book and picked up Marco's mobile. If it was time to go back to the real world, she'd better start dealing with it.

There were several texts, mostly people offering her their condolences over Marco's death. There was a voicemail too, from her landlord, complaining that the flat had been broken into and most of her and Marco's things had been destroyed. The man didn't know about Marco's death or any of what had been going on so he was understandably annoyed that the door the flat had just been left open and there was no sign of his tenants. He was shouting about binning their remaining possessions and keeping their deposit … even of setting lawyers onto them for damages.

Phoebe steeled herself to call him back, though it used up most of the credit on the mobile. She explained that Marco had been killed and she had gone away for his funeral. The man, who was a decent fellow really, instantly apologised for the message he'd left her. He said not to worry about the damage to the flat, he'd get it sorted out before she came home, but to be aware that most of their possessions were wrecked. Even her wedding dress had been shredded. Phoebe realised sadly that she could never go back to the flat. Not just because the demons would look for her there, but because she just couldn't face it. She explained that to the landlord, who seemed to understand. He offered to pack up any of their things that could be salvaged, and dump the ones that couldn't, to save her from having to go back and see her vandalised home. She asked him to send what remained to James's address, thanked him and put the phone down.

'That's it,' she announced, 'I'm homeless. Now what do I do?'

'For tonight, you sleep,' said Fen. 'We'll say here to protect you.'

Phoebe knew that with no sign of the demons, as yet, he was really staying to comfort her, so that she didn't have to feel alone.

'Thank you, Fen,' she said, beginning to feel tired. 'Fen … that's an odd name. What does it mean?'

'It's short for Defender,' he replied. 'Because that's what I'm here to do … defend you and the baby. And I will. I give you my word. I'll defend you with the last drop of my blood.'

Saraf stared at him, wide eyed. In a few days he'd gone from being totally disinterested in protecting anybody, to feeling completely committed to his charge, and now to her baby.

'Why can I hear you? I could hear you, but not Saraf, at the hospital, and at the flat, when I wasn't supposed to,' asked Phoebe, sleepily, settling back against her pillows.

It was a good question, one that Fen had wondered about too. He'd even asked Celeste, who explained that he was distantly related to Eskarron, they were from the same flight, or division of angels. Perhaps that was why Phoebe could hear him when she shouldn't have been able too; the girl had a remote connection with him. Which meant that she hadn't been able to hear Saraf's voice, because the young angel was from a different flight of angels, with no connection to Eskarron at all.

Thankfully Phoebe fell asleep before Fen could come up with a sensible explanation. He couldn't tell her the truth, and angels aren't particularly good at lying. Phoebe dozed off, reassured by the angels' presence, and feeling less alone in the world than she had done when she came off the phone to her landlord. She found she was beginning to think of Fen, and Saraf, as friends. It was an oddly comforting thought.

As Nonna Battista passed the door of Phoebe's room on the way to go to bed herself, she noticed that the light filtering out around the doorframe had a pure whiteness that was nothing to do with the soft electric lamps in the room. She paused to listen, and thought for a moment that she could hear voices, but they were so faint that she might have imagined them. She knew she wasn't imagining the light though. It had a purity, a brightness, that the old lady could only associate with something holy, and she was thankful.

She had a strong faith herself, and she was glad to think that Phoebe was under some kind of protection, even if the girl didn't seem to have had any belief herself, before Marco's death.

Nonna Battista went to bed and said her prayers for Phoebe and for the baby knowing that she herself wouldn't be able to offer them help for very much longer.

30

Phoebe set off with Giovanni the next morning, having promised Nonna not to stay out too long or do too much. The girl thought Nonna Battista herself wasn't looking very well, but the old lady had brushed off her concerns, putting her frail appearance down to old age and grief.

'Go with Gio,' she had instructed. 'See some more of de city. You can tell me all about it when we both get 'ome. Now, go, *figlia,* with my blessings on you and de *bambino*.'

Giovanni drove them first to the Coliseum, explaining that it would be better to get there early, before the place was too full of tourists. Phoebe pointed out that she was a tourist herself, but Giovanni laughed.

'A tourist with a local is not a tourist,' he said. 'She is a guest.'

'Why do you know Nonna Battista so well?' Phoebe asked as Giovanni parked the car on a side road. 'You seem very at home at her house. I know you were friends with Marco, but …'

'I used to stay there in the school holidays,' Giovanni answered, 'The shorter ones anyway. It wasn't practical to fly round the world to see my parents all the time, so Nonna Battista took me in. She and Marco … they became my family.'

They both fell silent. Today would have been her wedding day. They both knew it, but neither wanted to mention the date, or speak too much about what they had lost. Giovanni was determined to make Phoebe smile at least once that day. He felt it was the least he could do for his best friend. Marco would have wanted her to find some happy moments.

The Coliseum was getting busy by the time they arrived, but again they managed to skip the queues, this time because Giovanni was a police officer, with a very charming smile, and somehow got them waved in through a different gateway to the one where most of the other visitors were lining up to go in.

The place was so much bigger than Phoebe had imagined, and from the platform they were standing on it was possible to see all the tunnels that ran under the floor where the gladiatorial battles had taken place. There were walls supporting the floor, and cells where prisoners would have been kept and places for wild animals, with ramps to drive them up and into the stadium. Towering above all this were tiers of stone seats, including a section where the Emperor would have sat, ready to give the signal which would mean life or death to whoever was on the floor of the arena.

Although it was possible to climb up to the other levels, the heat made Phoebe feel tired at the thought of it and after taking a few photos, which was still a strange thing to do without Marco, the girl was ready to move on.

'If you wish to get out of the sun,' smiled Giovanni, 'We'll go to St Clemente's. But first, let me buy you an ice-cream. You cannot come to Rome and not taste proper gelati. Besides, it will give you a chance to sit down and have a rest.'

Phoebe welcomed the idea and the two of them sat outside a café on the shady side of the road, tucking into their ice creams.

'Tell me about St Clemente's, then,' she asked. 'Apart from it being on Marco's list, I've never heard of it.'

'That is because you are not a Roman.' Giovanni grinned. 'It is off the beaten track, even though it is so near the Coliseum. We can walk from here. It will take us less than five minutes. Did you bring a coat, or a jumper? There are levels beneath the church. If you like history, it is very exciting, but also rather cold.' Phoebe nodded. She had thrust a cardigan into her shoulder bag before they set off.

'Ready?' said Giovanni, standing up.

Seeing that Phoebe was looking a little tired already, he offered her his arm as they walked along the street. Again, the gesture reminded her of Marco, and she had to hold back the tears.

When they walked into the Basilica of St Clement, Phoebe took a deep breath. It was stunning. It had been built in the twelfth century, according to Giovanni, and behind the altar there was an incredible mosaic, mostly made up of golds and blues and reds, covering the whole wall. The mosaic was of Christ on the Cross, which was depicted as the Tree of Life, nourishing all living things: birds and animals and plants, with sheep below, saints above, and looking down from the highest level, angels.

Phoebe imaged that Fen and Saraf must be somewhere nearby, and could picture the little angel's delighted face when she saw this. Phoebe herself stood and stared at it in admiration for ages, particularly enjoying a rather lugubrious looking lion peering down from the top of the mosaic, until Giovanni tugged at her arm, explaining that there was much more to see. He dragged her through the little shop, where Phoebe again insisted on stopping to buy postcards, as photographs weren't permitted in the basilica. Then Giovanni led her to a ticket booth and paid for them both to go down into the lower level.

As they descended the steps Giovanni explained, 'Below is the original Basilica, built in 392 AD, and below that is a first century structure, used at a Mithraic Temple, and beyond that are sections of what is thought to have been the Roman mint.'

The lower they went the more pleased Phoebe was that Giovanni had warned her to bring a jumper. She pulled it on and clutched it tightly around herself as they descended into the deeper levels.

The fourth century basilica was decorated with frescoes and sculptures, and Phoebe was fascinated by how vast the underground structure was. Then Giovanni led her further down, through layer after layer of the ancient city, and Phoebe could almost feel the past pushing down on her. They stepped out into an ancient Roman house, which led to the Mithraic temple.

Since that area was crowded with tourists listening to a

guide, Giovanni hurried her along to the section that had been the mint. The fine arches were impressive, and nearby she could hear the gurgling of an underground stream. It amazed her that all this had been hidden below the ground for centuries, until years of excavations had revealed it.

Hearing the group of tourists move away up the staircase, Giovanni led Phoebe back to the temple. It was dimly lit by electric lights but Phoebe could see stone benches down either side of the low vault. At the far end there was a small statue, and in the centre an upright stone pillar, carved with an image of Mithras, sacrificing a bull to the god Apollo.

Phoebe absorbed the atmosphere in complete silence, since all the other visitors appeared to have gone. She started to shiver, sensing something nearby in the shadows ... or rather several somethings. It occurred to her too late that while sight-seeing in crowded places might be safe enough, going deep underground with only Giovanni to protect her might not have been wise. After all, he didn't know there was anything to protect her from, and she couldn't tell him. She looked round, hoping to catch a glimpse of Fen or of Saraf. Surely, they must be nearby? But all she could see when she glanced over her shoulder were five ugly, bulky shapes.

The demons were there, and Phoebe realised too late that the creatures had planned their ambush well. They were between her and the steps that lead to the level above. Worse than that, they were across the entrance to the temple, trapping her and Giovanni in the ancient, narrow space. Phoebe let out a cry, and Giovanni turned to see what she was looking at. The policeman struggled to believe his eyes. It appeared that there were five hideous demonic looking creatures behind them, and they were getting ready to attack.

31

Giovanni instinctively thrust Phoebe behind him as the demons closed in, trying to use his body to shield hers, and wished he had some kind of a weapon. Being off-duty, he hadn't brought his police handgun, and the only thing close enough to grab was a fist-sized lump of rock, which was hardly going to be enough to protect them against these horrors.

Seeing how well their trap had worked the demons were slavering in expectation of getting their claws and their teeth into the humans. They couldn't wait to tear them apart and feed on their flesh and blood and swallow their soul-lights. As they moved forward, they began jostling each other for the best position to get to Phoebe, and be the first to drink her special blood. The entrance into the temple was not wide enough for the five demons to move forward together, making their vying for position even more critical.

At that point Fen and Saraf caught up with Phoebe, having become separated when the angels were dodging groups of tourists. Fen's heart sank when he saw the demons. Five of them against two angels was not encouraging, especially when the demons were between him and Phoebe. Still, his job was to protect the girl, and that was what he was determined to do.

'Looking for a fight?' the angel called out, so loudly that his voice echoed round the underground chambers. The demons were momentarily startled and three of them looked round, but Dread and Dire remained focused on their human prey.

Saraf drew her cross out from beneath the neck of her robe, and Fen, though concentrating on the situation, made a mental note to ask her why she wore one: it wasn't as if angels needed reminding about what *He* had done for humans, nor had they any need to use jewellery as a statement of faith. Nonetheless, he was glad at that moment that she was still carrying it. He dived forward trying to grab the demon who was nearest to him, while cursing himself for having relaxed too much since their arrival in Rome. He should have been prepared, armed himself with things that could deter the demons.

Daunt, the creature he was grappling with, was clawing at Fen's face with one hand, while with the other he reached behind Fen's back, twisting one of the angel's wings painfully. Saraf dived forward, thrusting the cross against the demon's face, and the holy object caused the creature's skin to burn and blister. 'Depart,' commanded Saraf, 'In the name of the Father, Son and Holy Spirit.' A puzzled look came over the demon's face and he loosened his hold on Fen, but he did not depart. He couldn't, for since he was there in physical form, his essence was unable to leave without causing his own death ... even though the desire to obey Saraf's powerful command was strong.

Fen was amazed at Saraf's determined approach, given that most of the time she couldn't concentrate on anything for long. Looking past the demon he'd been fighting he saw the others were closing in on Phoebe and Giovanni, and tried to force his way towards them, but couldn't push his way through the other demons.

'Your bag,' Saraf shouted to Phoebe. 'Look in your bag!'

Giovani was looking completely bemused. Now he could see angels as well as the hideous creatures that were trying to attack them, since Fen and Saraf were too busy tackling the demons to control the speed of their wingbeats. Remaining invisible wasn't a priority just then, whatever the consequences later.

Phoebe, however, reached her hand into her shoulder bag and dug down until she could feel a plastic container. She hadn't put it there, but guessed that one of the angels had. When she pulled it out, she found it was a spray bottle, and correctly assumed it had been filled with Holy Water. Gripping it tightly the girl began to squirt it into the eyes of the demons, one of whom now grasped Giovanni's throat. This was the creature Phoebe recognised from the attack on her flat, the night after Marco's death.

Distracted by the pain, Dread released the young man, shoving him to the ground, then he reached out his claws towards Phoebe, slashing at the arm she was using to hold the spray bottle. The jumper she was wearing protected her skin a little, but Dread's claws still cut into her flesh, drawing blood, and the demon paused to savour the taste as he licked it off the tips of his claws. He hissed, and looked at Phoebe in wonder. Now he knew what made her blood special, and why it had had such an effect upon the imp, Glint.

'Angel blood,' he whispered, 'She's one of the children of Eskarron.'

He reached out and slashed at her again, determined to get more of her blood, even if the Holy Water she was defending herself with prevented him from getting much closer. The other demons, who had been grappling with Fen and Saraf, turned and stared at Phoebe, as the implications of what Dread had said sunk in.

'Don't kill her now, then,' Dire announced. 'She'll be more use to us if we take her into the Darkness and kill her there.'

Dread turned to his fellow demon, and savagely began to claw at Dire's eyes and throat.

'Don't tell me what to do,' shouted Dread, continuing his vicious attack. 'She's mine, I found her, and I'm going to drink her blood myself ... all of it, whenever I want to, and wherever I want to.'

The other demons stepped back, suddenly more afraid of Dread than of the angels they were battling with. At least angels played by the rules, but Dread seemed completely unpredictable. They had already seen him kill one demon, back in Stow, and none of them wanted him to be his next victim. Dire was screaming, as Dread's claws tore across his eyeballs, blinding him.

Giovanni scrambled to his feet, grabbed the rock he'd noticed earlier and brought it down hard on the back of Dread's head.

For a moment everyone in the temple was silent, except for Dire, still whimpering in pain.

Dread turned slowly to face the young man, and Phoebe squirted more Holy Water into the demon's eyes. Dread shrieked and Fen took the opportunity to force his way between the other demons and reach Phoebe's side. The angel started to drag her and Giovanni forward, trying to get them past the distracted demons and towards the stairs up to the next level, but the demons began to attack them again, although Dread was struggling to see out of his blistered eyes and Dire had collapsed to the ground, wailing.

Phoebe tried to squirt more Holy Water at the other demons, but only a few drops came out: the bottle was empty.

Now their only remaining weapon against the demons was Saraf's cross, but that could hardly protect them all at once. By pulling Phoebe and Giovanni out of the temple area and towards the stairs, Fen had enabled some of the demons to get behind them. Now Fen and the two humans were surrounded by four demons, who were closing in to attack once more.

32

There was a clattering sound at the top of the staircase, and they heard the voice of one of the tour guides explaining to her party of visitors what they were about to see when they reached the level below. Of course, she was telling them about the Mithraic Temple and the Roman Mint. She had no idea she was leading the tourists into a pitched battle between demons and angels, with human lives at risk in the middle of it all.

Saraf suddenly charged up the stairs, adjusting her wingbeats to become invisible. She cannoned into the tour guide, grabbing the rolled up, multicoloured, umbrella that the guide usually waved in the air so that her groups had something to follow in crowded areas. Opening the umbrella Saraf charged down the stairs, using it as a weapon to knock into the demons, sending them sprawling in all directions. Fen used the few moments she'd gained them to chivvy Phoebe and Giovanni up the stairs.

'Wait for us up in the Basilica, Phoebe,' shouted Fen. 'The demons will be weaker up there, if we can't deal with them all down here.'

Phoebe took Giovanni's hand and they hurried up the stairs, past the confused tour guide and her party, and on up through the building until they reached the top level, where Phoebe dragged Giovanni over to one of the pews to sit down. They were both shocked and dishevelled and needed a few minutes to collect their thoughts. Phoebe hoped she'd get at least a little peace before having to deal with anything else. She was wrong. The demons might not be giving her any trouble for the moment, but the same couldn't be said of Giovanni. He had questions. Lots of questions.

'What's going on?' Giovanni asked, turning to look Phoebe in the eyes. 'There were angels, and ... other things down there. They were trying to attack you. It was personal ... and what were they saying about your blood?'

Phoebe didn't know where to start with answering his questions, or even if she should. The fewer people who knew the better. That was what the angels had told her. But Giovanni had already seen them, just as she had, the night she had found Fen and Saraf protecting her from the demon when her flat was attacked. If he already knew, did it matter what else she told him? And it would be so good to be able to talk to another person about what was happening.

Several levels below, the angels and demons were scattering as the tour guide led her party down the stairs to the temple.

'If anyone sees my umbrella,' she was saying, 'Please let me know. I've no idea how I came to fall over and fling it into the air like that.' By the time the group had reached the bottom steps there was no sign of anything strange going on. The umbrella was abandoned on the floor at the entrance to the temple, though some of its spokes were broken. The angels had quickly become invisible to human eyes and hurried up the stairs to catch up with Phoebe and Giovanni, while the demons had tucked themselves into dark corners to avoid being noticed. The group of tourists was much too large to attack: better to hide until they could find the girl again. Anything else was wasted energy since she was the one they wanted: now more than ever.

Up in the Basilica Phoebe had filled Giovanni in on as much as she could. After a few minutes he lent back in the pew, and stared up at the religious mosaic in front of them.

'So all of it is true,' he said softly, after a few moments silence, 'Everything I learned as a child. Everything I put aside as an adult. All of it is true.'

'I don't know about that,' said Phoebe. 'I never learned anything much about religion, though Marco believed, I think. I only know the bits I've come into contact with since he died. I don't understand much about anything else.'

'I'd have thought meeting angels and ... demons ... might give you a bit of a clue,' said Giovanni, raising an eyebrow at her.

'What about?' answered Phoebe.

'That there is more to life than either of us thought?' grinned Giovanni. 'Marco would have been so excited about this.'

'He would, wouldn't he?' Phoebe replied, smiling.

Giovanni glanced down and noticed the cuts on her arm, visible through the slashed jumper. The bleeding had stopped, but the wounds looked sore and red.

'I should take you to a hospital,' he said, feeling guilty that he hadn't thought of it before.

'No,' said Phoebe. 'It's just a few cuts and scratches. I'll put some antiseptic on them when I get back to Nonna Battista's house ... if we can go back there.'

'We can,' said Fen's voice, softly, from behind them. Both angels were making an effort to remain invisible in the crowded basilica, although they were allowing their voices to be heard by both Phoebe and Giovanni. 'But not for long. You'll need to pack and say your goodbyes. Then we'll have to be on the move. That house is the first place they'll look for you.'

'So, it isn't over then?' she asked. 'You didn't kill the demons?'

'It's harder than you think,' Saraf muttered, huffily. 'They really don't die that easily.'

'Come on,' said Fen. 'We'd better get going.'

'Of course,' said Giovanni, standing up and helping Phoebe to her feet. 'But shouldn't we introduce ourselves first?' Fen and Saraf looked at each other and groaned ... another cat let out of another bag! And they'd probably be the ones trying to deal the consequences, whatever those might be.

'I'm Fen, this is Saraf,' the angel announced more briskly than usual. 'Now can we just get you both out of here before the demons catch up with us again.'

Giovanni nodded, and glanced at the mosaic again in wonder, before heading for the entrance.

'Do I really have to say goodbye to Nonna Battista?' Phoebe

asked sadly. 'She feels like family now.'

'I'm sorry, Phoebe,' said Fen gently. 'But yes, for the moment, anyway. I know it's hard, but we're only trying to keep you safe. You and the baby.'

The tourists stayed down in the Mithraic Temple for what seemed like ages to the demons, who were impatient to follow Phoebe. By the time that group had left another had arrived, and the demons had to wait as various visitors came and went, before eventually it was deserted enough for them to come out of hiding.

Arguments rapidly developed amongst the demons about their best course of action. Dread was surprised to find that the other demons resented his attack on Dire.

'What does it matter?' said Dread casually. 'What's one demon, more or less, when we're about to be the most powerful creatures in the Darkness. If we go back having drunk angel blood, no-one will be able to stand against us.' Of course, he didn't mean words like 'we' and 'us', but he needed the other three demons, for now anyway, to help him defeat the angels and get hold of Phoebe. In fact, it would be useful to have as many demons as possible. 'Where is Dire anyway?' The other demons glanced around, but couldn't see the injured creature anywhere. They began to hunt and found him curled up in a hollow under the stone benches in the temple. As they dragged him out into the light, they could see the wounds on his throat, and the gashes Dread had inflicted on his eyes. Dire glanced around, sightlessly, reaching out imploringly for help from the others.

'Leave him here,' commanded Dread, ruthlessly. 'He's no use to us like that, and I don't want him slowing us down.'

'But how are we going to find the girl?' asked Daunt. 'Surely they won't go back to the old lady's house … not for long anyway. We've lost the trail, and have no way to find her again.'

'Really?' queried Dread, gloating. 'You've forgotten something. I got a taste of the girl's blood. Not enough to empower me, but enough to help me track her – for a day or two anyway, until the effect wears off. But we need to go at once.' Drear reached down a lumpy dark green hand and tried to help Dire up, but Dread tugged him away. 'Come on, I told you to leave him.'

The other demons looked at each other nervously, then shrugged and followed Dread up the stairs.

Once they were gone Dire pulled himself into a sitting position then began to feel around the floor with his clawed hands. At last he found what he was searching for: a damp spot where a few drops of Phoebe's blood had splashed onto the ground. Crouching down, Dire began to lick up the blood with his tongue. After all, if there really was angel blood in her veins, perhaps it would help him heal. More than that, it might mean that he too could track the girl. That would mean he could follow his fellow demons. Because right now he was much more concerned with catching up with Dread and getting his revenge than he was in any human ... whatever blood was running through her veins.

33

Giovanni led Phoebe and the angels back to his car. Since there was no longer any point in being secretive around the policeman, the angels squeezed into the back seat, while Phoebe sat in the front. As Giovanni cut through the traffic in the middle of Rome, he couldn't help glancing in his rear-view mirror, and staring at his winged passengers, both of whom looked battered, tired and worried. Looking over at Phoebe, he was amazed by how calm she seemed about it all. He knew that she'd had longer to get used to all of this, but still …

Giovanni particularly admired the way she hadn't panicked during the demon attack, using the Holy Water in its bottle as efficiently as he would have used his service weapon, if he had had it with him. When he had first met Phoebe, he had almost wondered what Marco had seen in her, but now he understood. She had spirit and courage and a sense of humour that would have appealed to his best friend … that could have appealed to him, under other circumstances.

'Those … creatures … said something about Phoebe having angel's blood,' stated Giovanni, catching Fen's eye in the mirror. It was Saraf who answered him.

'An angel fell in love with a human female and was allowed to stop being an angel, and marry her. Their descendants have angel blood,' she explained. 'It's supposed to have special properties.'

'Like what?' Phoebe asked. 'Let me guess … you can't explain in case it makes things worse.'

'It probably would,' agreed Fen, 'But to be honest, we don't know what's special about it.'

He leaned back in his seat, and closed his eyes, ending the conversation.

They reached Nonna Battista's house in record time, and Fen

breathed a sigh of relief. All he had to do now was get Phoebe to pack quickly and say her goodbyes, then get her away from Rome, before the demons caught up with them. But as they entered the house, they realised that something was wrong.

For a start, the front door was slightly open, and when they made their way to the kitchen the room looked as if it had been burgled by very untidy but not particularly destructive robbers.

'Imps,' said Fen and Saraf, at exactly the same moment, looking round at the mess. 'This must be the consequence of Giovanni seeing us and learning what was going on,' added Fen.

Since the demons had been the ones attacking, and the angels had had to become visible while trying to protect him and Phoebe, the rules had been broken unintentionally. However, Phoebe filling Giovanni in on what had been going on, and the angels talking to him afterwards had been slightly more of an issue.

'Just a couple of them, I think,' added Saraf, glancing round. 'They haven't been very destructive, just annoying.'

'We should be able to get rid of them quickly enough,' agreed Fen. 'We'd better do that right away, before they upset Nonna Battista.'

'Where is Nonna?' asked Phoebe, nervously, just as Giovanni walked into the kitchen after checking out the other rooms downstairs.

'No sign of trouble anywhere else,' he announced. 'What?' The others looked at him, worried.

'Have you seen Nonna Battista?' Fen asked him. Giovanni slowly shook his head. The old lady was usually in the kitchen, preparing food. If she wasn't there, where was she?

Giovanni sprinted up the stairs two at a time, sticking his head in each room in turn, but found no signs of Marco's grandmother, nor of any disturbance. The was only one room left to check … Nonna's bedroom. He tapped lightly at the door, and it swung open.

There was Nonna Battista, lying on her bed, unmoving. He hurried over and shook her gently.

'Nonna? Nonna, wake up,' he said softly. 'It's Giovanni.

Nonna?' There was no reply.

By this time the others had joined him and were standing around the bed.

A choking sob escaped from Phoebe, and tears pricked at Giovanni's eyes. He reached out to take the old lady's wrist, searching for a pulse, but he already knew he wouldn't find one. Her skin was cool, and he thought she must have been dead for at least a couple of hours, maybe longer. He was used to seeing dead bodies as part of his work, but to see Marco's grandmother lying there felt so different. She was like family to him, just as Marco had been, and he didn't know how he would bear the loss.

'Did the imps do this?' Saraf asked. 'Did they kill her? If so, we will kill them!' Fen turned and stared at the usually gentle angel. He had never seen her look so fierce but then she, too, had grown fond of the old lady.

'I don't think so,' said Fen softly. 'Imps don't have the right, or the power, to kill people. Not deliberately, anyway.'

'Could they have frightened her to death?' Phoebe asked, horrified that Marco's grandmother might have died scared and alone.

There was a rustling under the bed and three imps crept out, looking scared themselves.

'We didn't do this,' muttered one.

'We just came up here to look for someone to annoy,' said another.

'She was like this when we found her,' added the third. 'Don't punish us for this … we only messed up one room.'

Realising that the imps were looking scared, not guilty, Fen began to pity them. They seemed inexperienced, perhaps this was their first time away from the Darkness, and the poor creatures were completely out of their depth.

Saraf was feeling less understanding.

'Do you swear you didn't hurt her?' she demanded.

The imps nodded, terrified by the fierce look on this avenging angel's face. Fen laid a hand on Saraf's arm.

'Think about it,' he said, 'Nonna Battista has been dead for a couple of hours, or more, so it can't have anything to do with these imps. It's less than two hours since the battle began, and even less than that since any of us did anything that could allow the imps through from the Darkness.'

'So she just ... died?' Phoebe asked sadly.

The angels nodded, and Giovanni picked up some papers that were folded up on Nonna Battista's bedside table. He glanced at them before handing them to Phoebe.

'She had another hospital appointment this morning,' Giovanni said sadly. 'I knew she was ill, but I didn't expect her to go so quickly. Then she saw her solicitor. She drew up a new will.'

Phoebe was staring at the second document, but since she couldn't read Italian it didn't make sense to her. Giovanni gently took back the papers and explained.

'She must have known she didn't have long. She changed her will. She has left me a few of Marco's things: everything else goes to you, Phoebe. She wanted to make sure you had a future.'

Phoebe reached out and softly touched Nonna Battista's cold hand. She knew she would feel grateful for this kindness later, but for the moment, she was numb with renewed grief for Marco, and his beloved grandmother. After a few silent minutes she turned to the angels.

'What do we do now?' she asked.

'We still have to get you away from here,' Fen replied, 'And quickly. You need to pack while we send these imps back where they belong.'

'But what about Nonna?' Phoebe queried, 'We can't just leave her here, alone.'

'No,' Giovanni agreed. 'We can't. I shall stay here and watch over her ... make the arrangements ... do everything that must be done. Then perhaps, I can follow you, help you with whatever you need, until these demons are ... dealt with.'

'Thank you, Giovanni,' said Phoebe solemnly.

Phoebe went to her room to pack, while Giovanni began the string of phone calls needed to report a death, and begin the arrangements for the old lady's funeral.

Meanwhile Fen and Saraf hauled the imps out into the

landing, and prayed them back into the Darkness, the creatures protesting rather less than they might have expected. The imps were just glad to be going home, painful as the process was for them, rather than being punished for murder by the angels.

34

Packing didn't take Phoebe long, though bursting into tears a few times slowed her down a little. Fen and Saraf went down to the kitchen and began clearing up the mess the imps had made. They didn't want to leave everything for Giovanni to deal with, he already had enough on his plate.

As they swept and tidied, Fen realised he still had some questions he wanted to ask his fellow angel, and this might be the last quiet moment they'd have for a while.

'Saraf, why do you wear a cross? It is a little … unusual for an angel?'

'My boy made it for me,' she answered with a proud smile. 'He was very clever. I wear it to remember him.'

This renewed Fen's curiosity about other people Saraf might have protected. She must have had other assignments in the hundreds of years between 'her boy' dying and now.

'Do you have anything else?' asked Fen. 'To remember other people.'

'No,' she replied crisply. 'I don't remember anyone else.' The way she said it seemed a little strange to Fen, as if there were people, but she didn't remember them. Which oddly made more sense than her not being given anyone to protect for hundreds of years.

Saraf turned away from him and seemed to be concentrating on scrubbing the old wooden kitchen table. Fen realised it was time to change the subject, before Saraf took the surface off the wood.

'It was clever of you,' he said, 'Putting a container of Holy Water in Phoebe's bag. Where did you get it from?'

'The water was from the font in the church, where Marco was buried,' Saraf replied, relaxing a little now Fen had asked her a question she was happy to answer. 'The bottle was from under the sink.' She pointed to the cupboard she'd raided for containers, smiling.

'Perhaps we should restock, while we have a chance,' suggested Fen, and Saraf nodded enthusiastically.

'I'll fetch more Holy Water,' she announced, and Fen realised she was bored with cleaning and wanted to do something else. He handed her a bucket from under the sink, and she bounced away in the direction of the church. He began emptying spray bottles of cleaners and liquid plant food, ready to fill them with Holy Water when Saraf returned.

'Thank you,' said Giovanni, from the doorway, carrying Phoebe's luggage. 'Nonna would have hated people to see her kitchen in such a mess. She was always very house-proud.' The young man looked around, then added 'Where is Saraf? Isn't it time for Phoebe to go? Before the demons get here?'

'Yes,' agreed Fen, 'as soon as Saraf gets back with some more Holy Water. I want to be better prepared next time.'

'Is there anything else you might need?' asked Giovanni. 'Take anything, Nonna wouldn't mind. The important thing is to protect Phoebe and the baby.'

Fen nodded, and looked around the house, collecting a bible, a candle and a small, painted icon. He wasn't sure what would work against such determined demons, but he wasn't about to be taken unawares again.

By the time Saraf was back with the Holy Water, and the containers filled up, Phoebe was ready to go and a taxi was waiting for them.

'I'm sorry I cannot drive you to the airport,' Giovanni explained. 'I feel I must stay here with Nonna. I do not want her to be here alone if the demons come and I must deal with all the ... business of her death. Promise me you will keep in touch, Phoebe, please? You have my number. I'll come and help you if I can.'

'I know,' said Phoebe, gratefully, giving him a parting hug. 'Thank you for everything, Giovanni.' The taxi honked it's horn outside, and it was time to go.

As the others left, Giovanni used the last of the Holy Water in the bucket to fill a spray bottle for himself. If the demons turned up at the house, he was ready to fight them and delay the creatures for a long as possible, so that Phoebe could get away.

As soon as Phoebe reached the airport, she used her open ticket to book onto the next available flight. The one that was about to take off was full, but space was found for her on the flight after that. Phoebe got the impression that they didn't want someone so pregnant to be delayed at the airport for too long, in case the baby came; although she didn't think that was a possibility yet.

Fen and Saraf travelled with her to the departure lounge, while keeping themselves unseen. It was crowded and brightly lit, with lots of security people around, which made it just about the most secure place for Phoebe to be.

Safe at last, at least for a while, Phoebe started shaking. The shock of the day's events kicked in, and she began to sob. She had already lost Marco, and now, on what should have been their wedding day, his grandmother was gone from her life too: just as the old lady had begun to feel like family. Even the fact that she didn't know if she'd see Giovanni again was upsetting. She'd come to think of him as her friend, although they hadn't known each other long. Now she was cast adrift, lost and homeless. It was good to be about to get on a flight, and put some distance between her and the demons who were after her blood, but she had no idea where to go once the plane landed.

Fen crouched in front of the sobbing girl. He didn't have to ask her what was wrong, he knew her feelings well enough by now, but he did have a suggestion for her.

'Why don't you call James?' he said, softly. 'Ask if you can stay at his, for tonight anyway, while you work out what to do next.'

'My phone is almost out of credit,' Phoebe replied, trying to get her tears under control. 'And I can't ask for his help again.'

'He's a good man,' Saraf whispered. 'He won't mind.'

Since she couldn't think of anything else to do, she accepted Fen's suggestion, although she was embarrassed about having to reverse the charges to make the phone call, especially from Rome. She was worried about costing James too much money, she had a feeling that vicars didn't earn much. However, when she did get put through to him, the conversation was reassuringly short.

'Of course you can stay here,' said James cheerfully. 'Give me your flight details and I'll pick you up from the airport.' .

It was settled. She was going back to Stow-in-the-Wold, briefly at any rate. She was surprised that James sounded so upbeat about her visit, given that he of all people, would know the kind of trouble that was bound to be following her. Phoebe smiled tentatively, feeling ever so slightly less alone. She still had a few people in her life that she could rely on, and a couple of angels looking after her. Things actually could be worse.

35

Dread and his diminishing band of demons made their way back to Nonna Battista's house, but even from outside Dread could sense that Phoebe was gone. The place was brightly lit too, with a car parked on the drive which had a 'doctor on duty' sign tucked behind the windscreen, and a dark, windowless van, pulled onto the drive behind that. They watched from the bushes as a body in a black bag was carried out on a stretcher, and placed in the van. Dread could see the young man on the doorstep ... the one who had dared to hit him with a rock. The demon was tempted to wait until everyone else had left, and attack him, as a punishment.

Satisfying as the idea was, Dread decided that he didn't have time to waste. He had only had a little taste of Phoebe's blood, and although he was confident, he could track her at the moment, he was concerned that the effect wouldn't last. They had to catch up with the girl before then.

'Where do we go now?' asked one of the demons.

'The airport,' Dread replied. 'I can feel she travelled in that direction, and her protectors will be keen to get her back to her own country as quickly as possible. Come on.'

James was waiting for them at arrivals when the plane landed. Fen and Saraf had travelled in the hold again, and re-joined Phoebe once all the luggage was unloaded. James welcomed all of them, shepherded them into his car, and began the long drive back to Stow.

'How did the funeral go, the Italian one?' he asked, conversationally, but looking at Phoebe's pale, drawn face he added, 'You look exhausted. You can tell me about everything in the morning. Just rest for now. Get some sleep if you can.'

Phoebe took his advice, leaning back against the headrest and closing her eyes. She slept fitfully on the journey, disturbed by memories of the day's events flashing into her mind.

By the time they reached the vicarage, Phoebe was wiped out and James and Fen had to help her into the house and up the stairs. She practically fell backwards onto the bed in the guestroom she'd used before, and sank into an exhausted, and mercifully dream-free sleep.

Dire was having to travel slowly, since his vision was still impaired, and the throat wound made any rapid movement extremely painful. He didn't bother to go to the old lady's house. He too had a faint sense of where Phoebe might be, having licked up some of her blood. He haltingly made his way to the airport, stopping to rest at intervals, determined to catch up with Dread and get his revenge.

By the time he arrived there, having clung to the underside of a bus for part of the journey, an experience he had no intension of ever repeating, as his head spikes had been dragged against the surface of the road, the other demons had already risked climbing into the hold of a plane. There was thick cloud cover and it was a late-night flight, so Dread had convinced them that it was worth the risk of being seen on the tarmac, in order to catch up with the girl, before his ability to track her wore off.

Dire, too, crept into the hold of a plane heading in the same direction, although he was hunting Dread, not the girl … not that she wouldn't be useful, and her blood was most definitely tempting, but first and foremost he was determined to destroy Dread, slowly and painfully. Everything else could wait.

Phoebe didn't emerge from her bedroom until the middle of the morning, the events of the previous day having drained her completely. She stumbled into the kitchen, bleary-eyed, to find Pam there, armed with toast and coffee, and insisting that Phoebe had a proper breakfast.

Pam was so motherly that she reminded the girl of Nonna Battista, and it was all Phoebe could do not to start sobbing again. However, she really didn't want her new friend to see her as someone who spent all their time blubbing, so she took a deep breath and tried to eat to please her.

By the time she'd finished, James had returned from a visit to one of his parishioners, and the five of them began to discuss the situation, and what to do next. This meant explaining to them what had happened in Rome, and when Phoebe became too choked up to speak, Fen and Saraf filled in the gaps for her.

'You're welcome to stay here for as long as you need,' James began, but Pam interrupted.

'Surely this is the first place those creatures will look for her,' she said firmly. 'We need to get Phoebe away. Take her somewhere different, where the demons won't be searching for her.'

'But I don't have anywhere to go,' said Phoebe, trying not to sound too pathetic.

'Just as well that I do, then,' Pam announced crisply. 'I've been intending to visit my sister for ages. She lives in Chester. It's a splendid city. Have you been there?'

Phoebe shook her head.

'Well, that's where we'll go. I'll tell my sister that you're my ... my Goddaughter. She'll be happy to welcome you too and she has plenty of space.'

'But what about the baby?' Phoebe protested. 'It's due soon.'

'There's a perfectly good hospital there. One of the best, in fact,' Pam added firmly.

'Are you sure you should be leading demons to your sister's house?' queried James. 'It seems like quite a risk to take.'

'Nonsense,' chuckled Pam. 'Emily is a Christian too. Worships at the cathedral. I can't imagine anyone better equipped to make a demon beg for mercy.'

'That's all very well,' said James. 'But what if they don't beg for mercy?'

'Then we'll kill them,' said Saraf, sweetly, as everyone else in the room turned to stare at her, shocked.

'You know that's harder than it seems,' stated Fen. 'Also, we're meant to be the good guys.'

'Good guys kill bad guys all the time – in films anyway' announced Saraf smugly.

Fen wondered when his fellow angel had had the time, or the opportunity, to watch lots of movies. He was beginning to think she must have protected other humans, even if she only ever talked about 'her boy.'

'You have a point though,' James said to Fen, 'What are we going to do if you can't kill them? Can we drive them back to where they came from?'

'The weak spot in The Hell-Fire Caves?' questioned Pam, 'But we closed that remember. Sealed it so that nothing else can come through from the Darkness.'

'Perhaps we need to unseal it, briefly, to drive these demons back through,' explained James, 'And then close it again, so they can't return.'

'That sounds like a plan,' agreed Fen.

'Right,' said Pam. 'I'll go and phone my sister. If it's all right with her, we'll leave tomorrow morning. It'll only take us a few hours to get to Chester.'

Now they had somewhere to go, Phoebe began to feel a little less frightened, although she had no idea how this was all going to end, or if it ever would. She was beginning to feel like she might have to spend the rest of her life hunted by demons. It wasn't what she wanted for herself, or her baby, but she couldn't see a way to make it stop. Not a good way, at least, and she refused to think about a bad ending: she had a child to protect.

36

'I do hope the demons don't turn up here again,' Phoebe said to James as she got ready to leave the next morning. 'I'd hate to cause you any more trouble.'

'Don't worry about it,' replied James. 'If they do turn up, I'll do my best to deal with them. And I'll be ready to go back to The Hell-Fire Caves and open the gateway if we need to.'

'Are you sure you don't mind me leaving my things here until I've found somewhere to live?' she asked. 'There'll be another box arriving soon too, from my landlord. He said he'd send anything that was left at the flat. Anything that wasn't ruined, anyway.'

'I don't mind at all,' James answered. 'I've got plenty of room here.'

'Thanks for topping up my phone credit, too,' said Phoebe, embarrassed. 'I haven't had a chance to do anything practical for days. I'm just so tired. All my body wants to do is sleep … but then I dream about Marco … .and Nonna Battista … and I'm wide awake again.'

'That's perfectly natural,' said James. 'Considering what you've gone through … what you're still going through.'

The doorbell rang, and James went to let Pam in. Phoebe rolled up the sleeve of her shirt, to see that the slashes on her arm were still red and sore and itchy. Perhaps when they got to Chester she'd try and get a doctor's appointment. She hadn't mentioned the cuts to James or Pam, as she didn't want to cause any more worry, but she was concerned that the wounds weren't healing. She quickly pulled her shirt sleeve down again as Pam walked into the room.

'All ready to go, Phoebe?' the older lady asked.

'Yes,' the girl answered, trying to look positive. 'I'd barely unpacked anyway.'

'I know this is terribly hard on you,' Pam said. 'Having to keep moving around, when all you want to do is rest, and have the time to grieve. But we can't think of any other way to keep you and the baby safe, and I promise you my sister will make you welcome.'

Phoebe and Pam said their goodbyes to James, and set off in Pam's car, heading towards the M5 and up to Chester. Phoebe was surprised to find that Pam was a pretty speedy driver, swinging the car round sharp bends on the country roads and putting her foot down hard on the accelerator when they reached the motorway. All thoughts of sleeping on the journey fled as Phoebe watched the scenery flashing by at an alarming rate, and wondered if she'd have been safer staying at James's and waiting for the demons to arrive after all.

The demons themselves were getting pretty hacked off. The plane they'd hidden in had landed at Stanstead airport, much further east than they'd expected, giving them a difficult journey to get to Stow-on-the-Wold, where Dread was convinced they would find the girl. The vehicles they'd managed to hide in all seemed to be going slightly north of their target, so by the time they climbed out of a wagon near Evesham, early that evening, Dread could sense that there was no point in continuing towards Stow: the girl was already on the move.

The other demons were fed up with the whole expedition. After all, they only had Dread's word for it that they were on the track of the girl with the angel blood in her veins. Or indeed, that that was what made her special, since Dread was the only one that had tasted it. They were tempted to rebel, and abandon the search, but they didn't know how to get back into the Darkness, nor did they want to make Dread angry. They had seen how savage he could be to other demons, and none of them wanted to annoy him and become his next victim.

In the end they just had to accept Dread's insistence that they change direction, and try to find a lorry that was heading north to hide in, but first they would have to wait until it got dark. The lorry they had climbed out of was collecting a load from a busy industrial park and getting seen would only complicate things.

Dire had had a better journey and reached Stow early that morning. He arrived in time to see Phoebe drive off with Pam, but was not too worried about having missed her. Phoebe's value to him now was as a way to locate Dread. Once he'd extracted his revenge, he could think about how he might use the girl. For the moment he was content to wait for a few hours to see if Dread and the other demons turned up at the vicarage, or if they, too, had realised that Phoebe had gone elsewhere. When evening came, and the demons didn't, Dire began his journey north.

The trip to Chester didn't take as long as Phoebe had expected, perhaps because of Pam's enthusiastic driving style. Even so, it was a relief when they pulled up outside an old Victorian semi-detached house in the outskirts of the city.

As soon as they stopped, Pam's sister, Emily, flung the front door open and made both her guests welcome.

'Come on in,' she said with a grin. 'I've got some home-made soup simmering on the stove. I'm sure you're ready to eat.' Emily was chattier than Pam, but Phoebe could see the similarity, not just in their appearance, but in the way they both accepted her and made her feel like part of the family. It was a little difficult not being able to be honest about why Phoebe was there, and the danger she was in, but Pam had been clear in the car on the journey to Chester that Emily didn't know about Pam undertaking certain tasks on behalf of angels, when needed, and that that aspect of things was best left unspoken.

All that Pam had told her sister was that Phoebe, who was pregnant, had recently lost her fiancé just before their wedding, and that Pam thought a change of scene would be good for her. If Emily looked a little surprised at just how pregnant the girl was, she was too polite to say so. Phoebe tucked into her bowl of soup, and let the sisters have a good catch up, without contributing much to the conversation.

'I expect you're tired after your journey,' said Emily when the meal was over. 'Do you want to lie down and rest, or go for a stroll and get some fresh air?' Phoebe opted for a stroll, if only because she couldn't face trying to sleep and having nightmares again.

Fen and Saraf, who had flown up to Chester, had been waiting outside the house. They could hardly go in and risk Emily catching a glimpse of them, so they had agreed to stand guard in the garden and only enter the house if Phoebe was in immediate danger.

They were a little surprised to see her going out with Pam and Emily so soon after her arrival but reasoned that the demons wouldn't have caught up with her yet.

'It'll be nice for her to see part of the city,' said Saraf, 'Chester is so beautiful.'

'Is it?' asked Fen, curious once more, 'So you've been here before? Were you protecting someone who lived here?'

Saraf turned away and inspected some honeysuckle flowering on a bush in Emily's garden, before starting to follow the others along the road towards the city centre. Fen, frustrated that Saraf had avoided answering his questions again, set off after them.

37

Emily lived near Grosvenor Park and automatically led her guests in that direction.

'It's the shortest way to get into the city from my house, and much the prettiest,' she explained, pointing out some of the landmarks on the way. They wandered slowly along wide paths between trees and lawns and walked under beautiful sandstone arches. 'These are ancient,' Emily announced. 'They've been moved about a bit, but now they're in their final positions. The wider arch was from St Mary's Nunnery. 13th century, I think … and the plainer arch was from St Michael's Church. This is a lovely old Victorian Park and there's the statue of Richard Grosvenor. He was the Marques who donated the land for the park and paid to have it landscaped.'

'So he'd have somewhere grand to put that statue, I suppose,' said Pam, unimpressed.

'Nonsense,' said Emily crisply. 'That was paid for by public subscription, in gratitude for what he'd done.' She turned to look at Phoebe, and added. 'Sorry, am I sounding like a tour guide? I don't mean to, but it is lovely to be able to show people around.'

'And she does love her city,' Pam added with a grin. 'So let's wander on and show Phoebe a little more of it.'

'Would you mind if we went as far as the Cathedral?' asked Emily. 'I need to drop off some notes for the newsletter?' Both ladies looked at Phoebe with concern.

'I expect I can manage that.' Phoebe grinned. 'I'm pregnant, not sick … but I might need a rest before I can walk back.'

'I'll buy us all some tea and cakes,' Pam announced. 'There are plenty of nice tea and coffee shops.'

'How pregnant are you?' Emily asked Phoebe. 'I can never tell with people. Some mothers look huge when their baby is months off, and others hardly show at all.'

'I'm definitely showing,' laughed Phoebe. 'I've lost track of dates a little … since Marco … But the baby's due in … Oh, I hadn't realised! In about three weeks.'

'Then make the most of this visit,' smiled Emily, 'It might be the last freedom you have for a while.'

They wandered out of the park into the city, past the Roman amphitheatre and the new buildings opposite it, and into the older streets, where the shops were stacked on top of one another with walkways running on two levels. The black and white Tudor looking buildings where part of what drew people to the city, but Phoebe was even more impressed when she saw the Cathedral, jutting up into the sky ahead of her, covered with carvings of gargoyles.

'Grotesques,' whispered Fen into her ear as he walked invisibly beside her, 'You're thinking gargoyles but a lot of them don't carry waterspouts. So they're really called grotesques.'

'What is it with everyone acting like a tour guide today?' hissed Phoebe under her breath.

'He's only trying to be helpful,' muttered Saraf, offended. 'You don't need to get huffy with him.'

'Sorry,' whispered Phoebe. 'I'm just not in the mood for a lesson on architecture.'

'What was that?' Emily asked, while Pam nudged Phoebe to remind her not to talk to the angels in public. It was much too difficult to explain.

'I was just saying,' Phoebe answered, 'That's quite an impressive piece of architecture.'

'It is, isn't it?' replied Emily, as they reach the great wooden doors of the cathedral. 'Why don't you go in and sit down while I drop off my notes? I'll only be five minutes' and she hurried off towards the administrative area of the building.

Pam and Phoebe went into the main body of the cathedral, and Phoebe took a deep breath. It really was beautiful, and felt so peaceful. She sank down onto a pew, glad of a few moments to just be, and to think. After she'd absorbed the atmosphere for a while, she turned to Pam.

'It seems very busy here,' Phoebe remarked to her friend, as people scurried past, some of them preoccupied with their own business, but many seeming to be kind and friendly, taking an interest in each other and the visitors, and a few of them smiled at her in a sympathetic way. Phoebe even found herself smiling back.

'Of course,' her friend replied. 'Cathedrals generally are busy. There are always plenty of people around, not just during services, but all the time. There are tourists of course ... hundreds of those. But lots of people work here too, and some of them live just around the Abbey Green, on the other side of the building. In fact, it can be difficult to catch a few moments quiet in here, at certain times of day.'

A middle-aged man, his hair just starting to turn grey at the temples, and wearing clerical clothes, walked down the centre of the nave. Phoebe caught his eye and they exchanged smiles before he continued on his way, nodding in farewell. His smile was delightful, mischievous and kind at the same time, and something about him made Phoebe feel so welcome, so safe, that for the first time in days she allowed herself to feel hopeful for a few moments.

Phoebe stood up, wandering up the nave, between the choir stalls and into the Lady Chapel. Glancing at the ceiling she saw that it was covered with paintings of angels, looking golden and saintly. She nudged Pam and pointed at the images, and the two of them shared a smile. They both knew that the angels they were acquainted with rarely looked so calm and composed. Strolling back towards the great double doors, Phoebe stopped to glance at the service times, pinned to a notice board. There seemed to be so many services throughout the day; the building had been built for worship and that was still its main purpose. To Phoebe the whole place felt special. The atmosphere filled her with calm, and a sense of safety and peace. Maybe one day, she'd get to come back here: when she wasn't on the run.

'Even with everyone bustling about, it feels quiet,' Phoebe remarked, 'Better than quiet it's ... reassuring. It makes me feel a little more optimistic I suppose. Perhaps Fen and Saraf will find a way to put an end to all this ... get rid of the demons, so I can look after my baby in peace. Three weeks, Pam. It's due in three weeks. It's going to get harder and harder to keep running.'

'I'm sure you won't have to,' said Pam, trying to sound confident. 'The angels will find a way to get it sorted out before that.'

Fen and Saraf exchanged looks. It was all very well for Pam and Phoebe to rely on them, but they really weren't sure how to sort the demons out. Not permanently, anyway.

As she had promised, Pam brought them all tea and cakes on the way back to Emily's house. Phoebe sat at a table in the window, while Pam and her sister went to fetch their order. The seats were in the sunlight, and Phoebe began to feel too warm. Her arm was itching, and she eventually had to roll her sleeves up, so that its fabric stopped rubbing against the cuts.

Pam put a tray on the table and stared at Phoebe's arm sternly.

'When did that happen? And why haven't you been to a doctor?' Pam asked.

'It was in Rome, that last day,' Phoebe tried to explain to Pam without giving Emily a clue about what was really going on. 'I haven't had time since. I thought the cuts would just heal.'

'You obviously thought wrong,' said Emily. She glanced at her watch. 'We're a bit late to try and get you a doctor's appointment today, but first thing in the morning, we'll call the surgery that I go to, and get you seen as a visitor.'

Phoebe tried not to glance out of the window. She was pretty sure that Fen and Saraf would be outside, and even though she couldn't see them, she knew they would be cross with her for ignoring the wounds the demon's claws had inflicted. Which meant they'd be bound to start telling her off later, if they got a chance to talk to her without Emily being around.

Phoebe sighed. Her life seemed to be so much more complicated now, and she had no-one to share it with, except a couple of guardian angels, and an odd assortment of friends she hadn't even met a couple of weeks ago.

38

When the ladies had finished their tea, Emily insisted that they took a taxi home. Phoebe was looking rather flushed, and Pam and her sister were beginning to worry about the girl. Phoebe laughed off their concerns, but secretly she was glad not to have to walk all the way back. It was probably just the tiredness of pregnancy, but she was completely exhausted all of a sudden.

Once they were back at the house, Phoebe went up to her room to rest. As soon as she was alone, she got out her mobile phone and sent a text to Giovanni, asking how he was, and if there was a date set for Nonna Battista's funeral. As she had hoped, Giovanni phoned her back, and she found she was really pleased to hear his voice.

'How are you doing?' he asked her.

'I'm all right,' she replied, 'Just very tired. The baby is due soon. Oh, Giovanni, I don't know what to do. I'm staying in Chester for now. I'm with Pam, the lady you met in Stow. We're at her sister's but I can't keep running away. Soon I won't be able to run at all, and I can't dodge from place to place once the baby is born, either. We'll need somewhere to settle.'

'Perhaps you should come back here,' Giovanni suggested, 'Back to Rome, once the baby is born. You will have the house here, eventually. Nonna left it too you though you couldn't move into it yet. Not until all the legal aspects are sorted.'

'How are you coping?' Phoebe asked. 'I know how close you were to her. It must be hard for you, making all the arrangements.'

'It is always those who are closest who must do these things,' he replied. 'It is hard to lose her… especially so soon after …' he paused, unwilling to upset her.

'After Marco's death,' said Phoebe, forcing herself to finish the sentence for him. She had to get used to saying those words.

It was part of accepting that he was gone and she'd never see him again. That he'd never see the baby; and that was the worst thought of all.

'I wish I could come to the funeral.' Phoebe tried not to sound too weepy. 'Do you have a date yet?'

'This Friday,' he answered sadly. 'Most of the arrangements are made now, so it is just that period of waiting. Feeling I should do something, but there is nothing to done.'

Phoebe knew how that felt.

'Don't think of coming over,' Giovanni continued. 'She would not want it, with the baby due so soon. Also, it is better you keep away from the places those creatures might look for you.' There was a long pause, then Giovanni added, 'That did happen, didn't it? The demons, the angels … all of it?'

'It happened all right,' Phoebe confirmed. 'I still have the scratches to prove it.'

'Have those not healed yet?' he asked, sternly. 'You should have gone to a doctor.'

'I haven't had the chance, but I'll go tomorrow.'

'Promise me that you will,' he said. 'I don't mean to nag you, but Marco would want me to look out for you.'

Phoebe smiled, even though Giovanni couldn't see it. It felt as if Marco was still watching over her, through his best friend.

'All right, Giovanni, I promise I'll go to the doctor's tomorrow.'

'Good,' he replied, relieved. 'Who knows what kinds of infections a demon's claws might carry. I can't believe I just said that out loud.'

'I know what you mean,' Phoebe agreed. 'Knowing all this … stuff … but not being able to talk about it. At least, I can talk to the angels …'

'I can't believe you just said that out loud either,' Giovanni chuckled.

'I know,' said Phoebe. 'The world seems very weird at the moment. It's good we can talk to each other too. I'm really glad you found out, Giovanni, even though it did give you a shock.'

'So am I, I think. Well, I have to go, but keep in touch … and take care of yourself.'

'I will,' said Phoebe.

'I mean it,' her friend reiterated firmly. 'Please, be careful.' He hung up, and Phoebe stared at the phone for a moment, feeling a little lost.

It didn't take long for Dire to find a lorry to crawl into, and after only two changes of vehicle, he got to Chester shortly before midnight. He was beginning to find it harder to get a sense of where the girl was and was relieved when he located the house she was staying in before the effects of her blood wore off.

He could see a bit more than he had been able to after Dread had attacked him, but despite the fact that demons usually healed quickly, he was still struggling to make sense of the world around him though his lacerated eyes, and the wound on his throat kept opening up. Even the spikes on his head were oozing some foul-smelling goo. He tucked himself out of sight in the garden and settled down to wait.

He saw the three women turn out the houselights and head up to their bedrooms, and he saw the two angels fluttering up into the air to hover outside the bedroom window of the room he suspected the girl was in. Dire did nothing but watch. He still wanted his revenge and so patience was what he needed now. Dread was on his way; he was sure of that. And Dire would make him pay once he arrived.

Phoebe was just about to get ready for bed when she was disturbed by tapping on the window. She couldn't see anyone there, but she guessed it was either Fen or Saraf. Opening the window wide, she discovered it was both of them. The girl invited them in, although she was pretty sure they were about to tell her off. Oh well, she might as well get it over with.

'Let me see your arm, please Phoebe,' Fen said. With reluctance, Phoebe rolled up her sleeve and held out her arm for his inspection. It looked much worse than it had in the tea shop.

'That's bad,' Saraf added conversationally. 'All red and infected.' She looked more closely. 'Urgh! Are those wriggly things?'

Fen and Phoebe both leaned forward at the same time, knocking their heads together.

'Ouch,' protested Phoebe. She turned to Saraf, horrified, 'What do you mean 'wriggly things'? I refuse to have 'wriggly things' in my arm.'

'No, it's all right,' said Fen after taking a closer look. 'The infection is causing blisters, and the skin is rippling a little, but there aren't any creatures in the wound.'

Phoebe thought that was just as well. If they'd discovered living creatures in her arm, transmitted to her by the demon when it scratched her, that would have been more than she could cope with. As it was, she felt sick.

'You really do need to see a doctor, Phoebe,' said Fen, 'This is a nasty infection and you don't want it getting into your bloodstream.'

'Not when you're pregnant,' Saraf added, wandering over to the window.

Alarm spread through Phoebe's mind. She'd been so busy trying to keep one step ahead of the demons, to keep herself alive and protect the baby, that she hadn't even thought of a much more basic risk to the life she was carrying inside her.

'What should I do?' she asked Fen. 'I don't want to make the baby sick by leaving it 'til the morning.'

'You shouldn't go out now,' said Saraf, cheerfully, 'There are demons in the garden.'

39

From Evesham, Dread and the other demons had reached Chester fairly quickly, only needing to swap wagons once to complete the journey. Dread, too, was finding the girl increasingly hard to track, and was relieved to have caught up with her while he still could, which made it imperative for them to get hold of her as soon as possible. If she gave them the slip now, they'd might never find her again.

Dire watched from his hiding place in the bushes while Dread and the others argued about whether to attack the house and everyone in it at once, which was Dread's preferred option, or wait until the girl came out, which was what all the other demons wanted to do.

Of course, Dread won the debate: they were all far too scared of him to stand up against him in an argument. They'd all seen what he could do and Dire had felt what he could do, in person. It wouldn't be long now until he found a way to pay Dread back for every agonising wound.

'I think this is going to get nasty,' said Fen grimly. 'I'm sorry, Phoebe. I'm supposed to protect you from all of this. I've not done a very good job of it so far, have I?'

'I'm not complaining,' said Phoebe, gratefully, reaching up and giving her protector an unexpected kiss on the cheek. 'Given the circumstances, keeping me and my baby alive this long is impressive.'

Saraf hurried out of the room to wake Pam, and warn her that the demons had arrived.

'We'll do everything we can to keep you safe. Everything!' Fen stated, 'But if we can't, you need to remember, don't let them drag you into the Darkness alive. Better for you, and everyone else, to die here than there. And even if they cut you, don't let them drink your blood again.'

Fen felt tears starting to form in his eyes, and was angry with himself for feeling so emotional, and for having to give such grim advice. He was terrified that the demons would get hold of Phoebe, and he wouldn't be able to stop them. He was astonished to discover how much he had come to care for this brave young woman, in just a few days. Fen hadn't let himself become attached to any of his charges for over twenty years.

'How do we fight them?' asked Phoebe, determinedly. 'What can we use? We've come this far, let's not give up now.' She grinned, adding, 'I'd hate you to have my death on your conscience.'

Fen struggled to meet her eyes, since that was exactly what he was expecting to happen.

'Well?' said Phoebe, 'How do we fight?' Not that she felt like fighting, she was far too exhausted, but she wasn't a quitter either.

'I'm so proud of you,' said Fen. He smiled at the girl and she smiled back before rooting through her shoulder bag to find her mobile and phone James. They'd agreed that if things came to a head, they'd warn him to be ready to go and open up the gateway in The Hell-Fire Caves, in case any demons fled back there.

Promising that she'd let James know when he needed to set off, Phoebe pulled her camera out of her bag.

'What about light?' Phoebe asked as Saraf came back into the room. 'Would that put them off?'

'Try it,' said Saraf, moving to stand beside Fen at the window.

'Smile!' said Phoebe, jokingly, as she took a couple of photos to check that the flash was switched on, then edged between the angels to lean out of the window herself. Pointing the camera down into the moonlit garden, she took four more pictures. The flash illuminated the demons, who froze for a moment, then scurried out of if its range when they realised how uncomfortably bright the light was.

Dire grinned as he realised the demons were still arguing amongst themselves about the best way to attack the house and its occupants, while the people inside were obviously busy getting ready to defend themselves. This could be interesting to watch. He might as well sit back and enjoy it. He'd get his revenge on Dread when the time was right.

'We'll use fire,' Dread announced. 'It'll bring everyone out of the house. They'll be frightened and defenceless. Then we can grab the girl while the angels are trying to put out the flames.'

'The flames will show us up,' protested Drear. 'People will see us. They'll call the police.'

'Or the fire brigade,' added Daunt. 'We'll be overrun with humans in minutes.'

'We'll have grabbed the girl and gone by then,' growled Dread. 'Now gather up some firewood, and pile it in front of the door, or I'll set fire to one of you instead.'

Pam appeared in the doorway of Phoebe's bedroom, dressed and ready for action.

'Saraf woke me up. She said we're about to be under attack,' Pam spoke as calmly as if she was offering to make everyone a cup of tea.

Emily appeared just behind her, taking the sight of a couple of angels in her guest bedroom with remarkable calm.

'Nobody came and woke me up,' said Emily disapprovingly. 'Anyone care to tell me what's going on?'

The angels looked at each other and sighed. It couldn't be helped; they'd have to tell her.

'Demon attack,' said Fen, hoping to give as little as possible away.

'They're after Phoebe,' added Pam, for clarification. 'Sorry about bringing them here, we'd hoped they wouldn't follow us.'

'Why are they after Phoebe?' asked Emily, puzzled.

'She has angel blood,' Saraf announced gleefully.

'Great,' muttered Fen. 'More rules broken. Just what we need.' He leaned out of the window and said quietly, 'I'm sorry Emily, your front door is on fire.'

'Drat,' said Emily. 'Never mind, it needed repainting anyway and I never did like that colour.'

The others looked at Emily in amazement. She was taking this all rather well.

'That's my sister,' said Pam proudly. 'I told you she could handle it!'

'Shouldn't we do something about the fire?' asked Phoebe, puzzled that she seemed to be the only one concerned about it.

'Easy,' said Emily as she hurried off to get dressed. 'The bathroom is above the front door, shove the shower hose out of the window and aim down it at the flames.'

Fen hurried to do as she suggested, and soon the water was pouring down from the bathroom window, extinguishing the flames below. Emily reappeared, fully dressed, and hurried down the stairs.

'Now to get those horrors off my lawn,' she said and flicked a switch beside the front door. Jets of water sprung up from the lawn, and the demons jumped back in shock.

'You have a sprinkler system?' said Pam, incredulous. 'Why? You're in the North West! It always rains up here!'

'Yes, it does' replied Emily. 'But I thought it might be useful, if there was a drought. I never expected to use it for these purposes.'

Phoebe grinned as she realized that Pam and her sister were a pair to be reckoned with. Perhaps everything would be all right after all. They could just wait until morning and the demons would have to get out of sight.

Suddenly the pain in her arm worsened, and Phoebe dropped onto the bed, trying not to scream. Fen rushed over to examine the wound. In the last few minutes the infection had spread, down to Phoebe's hand and up to her shoulder. Her skin was swollen and inflamed, with blisters breaking out all over it. Pam looked over Fen's shoulder and tutted.

'She needs to get to hospital,' Pam declared. 'Right away.'

Nobody argued.

'But how are we going to get her out of the house?' asked Saraf.

40

Dread was getting frustrated. He'd expected to set fire to the door and have everyone rushing outside into the garden in minutes. Instead they'd simply put out the fire, and stayed snugly indoors. The demon tried to think about what his prey might do next. Every other time they'd been cornered, they'd broken free and run, so he just needed to find a way to stop them running. He looked around for inspiration, and found it.

Fen was pacing up and down, stopping every so often to touch Phoebe's shoulder reassuringly. Suddenly she screamed at his touch, and he knew they couldn't delay any longer. They had to get her to hospital.

'Pam,' he said, 'I'll distract the demons, if you and Emily can get Phoebe out to your car and drive her to hospital. Stay with her there, try to keep her safe. And don't come back here until the sun comes up. The demons tend to keep out of the way during the day.'

'What'll you be doing?' Pam asked.

'Saraf and I will attack the demons, and try to create a distraction, while you get Phoebe away,' Fen replied.

'What a pity we don't have any Holy Water,' said Emily, 'We could pour it into the sprinkler system. That would distract them all right!'

Fen turned to stare at her. 'Can we top up the sprinkler system from inside the house?'

'Of course,' replied Emily. 'The reservoir is in the downstairs cloakroom. I thought it would be nice to be able to fill it from inside in case …' she tailed off.

'In case it was raining?' finished Pam, shaking her head

in disbelief at her sister's irrationality.

'It seemed like a good idea at the time,' said Emily crestfallen.

'It's a brilliant idea,' Fen grinned. 'Especially since it just so happens that we do have Holy Water with us. Come on Saraf, let's go and set up the distraction.'

In a few minutes they were ready. There was Holy Water in the sprinkler system, just waiting to be turned on, and more in the spray containers that Pam and Phoebe had brought with them from Stow. Phoebe managed to stand up and Pam and Emily supported her down the stairs, Phoebe's shoulder bag flung over Pam's arm, along with her own handbag. Emily managed to look as neatly turned out as if she was heading to the Cathedral for a service, her coat tidily buttoned and a handbag firmly gripped in her free hand.

The sprinkler system was switched back on, and this time it was Holy Water that squirted onto the demons, driving them back in pain.

Dire watched in delight.

With the angels either side, armed with spray bottles, the group dashed out of the house and down the path to Pam's car then stopped, gazing at the slashed tires in horror.

'We'll take mine,' said Emily. 'I've got the keys in my handbag.' She looked towards where her car stood 'Oh no! My tires are flat too. They've slashed all the tyres of all the cars near the house.'

They were trapped.

The demons began edging their way around the water jets, trying to find a route that didn't get them burned too badly, and Fen realised there was no choice but to make a run for it. Emily and Pam were already helping Phoebe along the road, trying to put as much space as possible between themselves and the creatures. Fen and Saraf followed behind, spray bottles at the ready, to try and keep the demons at bay.

Emily led them into the park, hoping that there would be

more places to shelter in there than on the nearby roads. Soon the strange looking collection of people and angels were hurrying along the tree lined paths. The trouble was, Phoebe was in no state to hurry. The infection was weakening her and it was all she could do to put one foot in front of the other.

Dread was shouting at the other demons, urging them to ignore the blistering pain of the Holy Water, and just charge through it to chase after the girl, but the creatures were growing increasingly reluctant to obey him.

Dire watched, amused. He wondered if their disobedience would cause Dread to attack another of his so called allies, and it did.

Dread leapt forward, grabbed one of the other demons and hurled him onto the lawn, where the water from the sprinklers splashed onto his skin. Remarkably, after an initial scream of fear, the creature was silent, then it sat up and grinned.

'No more Holy Water,' the creature announced. 'This is just the ordinary type.' Of course, once the Holy Water in the reservoir had been used up, ordinary water had continued to flow into the system. The demons had just wasted several minutes avoiding being splashed by perfectly normal tap water.

Dread growled in frustration and chivvied the others out onto the road. They went in the direction that they'd seen the others take, but when they reached the end of that road, they turned to look at their leader.

'Which way did they go?' one of them asked.

Dread hesitated. He tried to sense the girl's location, but it felt as if his ability to track her had faded. He had the faintest sense of her, a little distance away, and led the group in that direction, but by the time they reached the entrance to Grosvenor Park, even that trace had faded. Would they have gone in there, or stuck to the roads, which at least were lit by streetlights? Dread really didn't know but decided to search the park first before hunting along the streets.

Hidden by shadows, Dire crept into the park after them.

Pausing to allow Phoebe a chance to rest for a moment, Fen turned to Emily.

'Where are we heading?' he asked.

'The Countess of Chester,' Emily answered.

Then, seeing the puzzled looks on everyone's faces, she added, 'Not the person … the hospital.'

'Is it far?' Saraf asked. 'I'm not sure Phoebe can walk much further.'

Phoebe felt like pointing out that she was still there, they could always ask her, but that would have required more energy than she could spare.

'It is a bit far,' Emily admitted guilty. 'It's some distance beyond the Cathedral.'

Phoebe's heart sank. She knew that she just wouldn't be able to walk that far. The pain in her arm was intense and moving made it feel worse. If it wasn't for the baby, Marco's baby, inside her, she'd be tempted to just lie down and let the demons attack her when they caught up with them. She suspected that would be pretty soon.

'Can you carry her?' Saraf asked Fen.

He tried lifting the girl but she was too heavy for him to keep her in the air for more than a few seconds. Saraf joined him, and together they could lift Phoebe up, but not carry her any distance. They lowered her gently back down onto the path.

'The river!' said Emily suddenly. 'If we can get down to the riverfront, there'll be taxis outside the pubs and restaurants.'

'At this time of night?' queried Pam, incredulous.

'Chester has a nightlife,' snapped Emily. 'Not like sleepy old Stow-on-the-Wold.'

'There's nothing wrong with Stow!' Pam said.

'Ladies!' Fen interrupted, 'Please can you have this debate some other time? Let's head for the river. Which way?'

'Through the park and down the road,' replied Emily, taking Phoebe's arm and heading in that direction. 'It'll be brightly lit down by the river too, which might discourage those horrible creatures. We'll be safer there.'

They had just reached the open area with the sandstone arches that Emily had been pointing out to them that afternoon, when they realised they weren't going to make it to safety.

They had walked under one of the arches and were heading for the next when they realised that the demons were crouched on top of it, waiting for them.

41

'You took your time,' said Dread, leaping down onto the ground in front of them. 'I thought you'd never get here.' The other demons dropped to the path beside him.

Fen and Saraf stepped in front of Phoebe, Pam and Emily, spray bottles at the ready. Fen turned to give Phoebe an encouraging smile over his shoulder, but for the first time the girl looked as if she didn't have any fight left in her.

'I'll fight for all of us then,' Fen thought to himself.

'What's the drill?' Emily whispered to her sister.

'Pray,' said Pam calmly. The two ladies stood either side of Phoebe and began to pray aloud. The demons started to close in as a pale light began to surround the three women, and the angels leapt forward to defend them, spraying the Holy Water into the demons' eyes, but Dread had expected that to happen.

As the creatures moved forward Dread grabbed one of his fellow demons and used him as a shield so that he could attack without getting burned himself. Leaving the other two demons to fight the angels, he charged towards the circle of light where Phoebe was standing between Emily and Pam.

Daunt and Drear leapt forward, straight into the spray of Holy Water that Fen and Saraf pointed at their eyes, but this time the creatures were determined to keep coming at them, however much it hurt. They wanted this battle over, the hunt had gone on long enough, and they rammed themselves against the angels, causing Fen to drop the spray bottle, and Saraf to lose her footing and land on her back on the lawn.

Dread, having established that the prayer light was stopping him getting to Phoebe, used the demon that was still struggling in his arms like a bowling ball, throwing the creature straight at Phoebe with such force that she was knocked over and the top half of her body landed outside of the circle of light. Dread sprinted round it to grab her and pull her away from the others. The demon who had been thrown at Phoebe climbed unsteadily to his feet, and threw himself at Dread, angry enough to fight his leader for a chance to taste the girl's blood.

Fen and Saraf were rolling on the ground, battling the demons that were clawing at them. Saraf suddenly stopped moving, and the demon she'd been fighting with assumed he'd beaten her and turned to attack Fen instead. With two demons on top of him, Fen was struggling, his face was cut and bleeding and some of the feathers from one wing were scattered on the path.

Dread was attempting to shove the other demon away from Phoebe while trying to get her blood for himself. He ripped at her swollen arm, and some of her blood spilled onto the grass. Phoebe yelled as his claws tore her flesh open, but she found the injury had relieved some of the pressure in her arm too. It has also broken through the drowsiness she'd been feeling and given her a new determination to fight back. She scrambled to her knees, and saw Pam and Emily moving towards her, trying to encompass her in their circle of prayer light, but the demon that had been thrown at her was blocking their route. She saw Emily raise her handbag and swing it around to connect with the creature's head. The demon fell to its knees, and Phoebe wondered what on earth the woman kept in there.

Saraf was on her feet running towards Pam and pointing at her handbag. Pam pulled a large bible out of it and threw it to the angel, who spun round and ran back to help Fen. She grabbed a fallen spray bottle and leapt onto the back of one of the demons that was attacking him, thumping the creature's head with the bible and twisting to spray the demon's eyes, forcing him to let go. Saraf was now running towards Dread, attempting to hit him with the bible too, but he dodged he attack.

'Use the words,' Pam called out, 'not the weight,' but Dread had already twisted round and grabbed Saraf, hefting her through the air. She landed in some rose bushes, and the thorns ripped her skin. She had lost her grip on the bible and had no idea where it had landed.

Saraf scrambled out of the bushes, with a couple of snapped

off roses still caught on her gown. Remembering the cross, she wore around her neck, she pulled it out and ran at Dread again, but he wasn't about to let her burn him with it a third time. He grabbed the chain it hung from, snapping it in two, and the cross fell onto the grass, where Saraf couldn't find it, though she did drop to her knees, trying to feel for it in the darkness. By now the demon that Emily had knocked out was back on his feet and charging at Dread once more. He tripped over the kneeling angel and fell head forwards cannonballing into Phoebe. This knocked her further away from Pam and Emily, who were trying to move towards the girl to protect her with their circle of prayer light but couldn't get past the raging demons.

With one of the creatures lifted off him, Fen struggled to his feet, trying to grapple the other one to the ground, but the first demon, Drear, charged back in to attack again. Fen was tiring, as the two demons clawed and punched him. Daunt gripped his wings, twisting them at the shoulder, causing Fen to scream in pain as he felt the wing twist out of its socket and flop uselessly behind his back. Drear was tearing at Fen's face with his claws, though Fen kept trying to twist out of range.

The trouble was, all the weapons at their disposal worked well against demons which had come through from the Darkness as an essence of evil, taking over a human victim and bending them to their will. Crosses and bibles, prayers and Holy Water could drive the demons out leaving them helpless, with nowhere to go but back into the Darkness. Fighting these creatures was different: they were here in their true, hideous form. They couldn't be driven out of their own skins and had no way to return to the Darkness. The angels' usual weapons could slow the creatures down, but they didn't seem able to defeat them.

Attempting to look beyond his own predicament, Fen glanced over at the others. Pam and Emily were still praying, but although surrounded by prayer light themselves, they couldn't move past the demons to get to Phoebe. Saraf was on her knees on the grass, and seemed to have lost interest in what was going on around her. Fen saw Dread grab the demon that had dared to attack him, and threw the creature against one of the sandstone arches, stunning him briefly.

Too far away for him to reach her, Fen could see Phoebe, her blood running down her arm, Dread poised to grab her and drink his fill.

The battle wasn't going the angels' way, and there was only one thing left that Fen could think of to save the girl. Using the last of his strength, he shoved the demon in front of him away for just long enough to reach down and grab a sharp sided stone from the edge of the path. He held it up to his own throat and yelled, to get the demons' attention.

'You want angel blood? Take mine!' Fen swiped the sharpest edge of the rock across his own throat, and his blood began to gush out. He had no idea what effect his blood might have on the demons … hopefully it would be less than they expected, much less than the effect of Phoebe's blood, which was made up of angel and human blood mingled together. He gave it willingly too. That might make a difference. He saw Phoebe's face, looking at him in horror, then her look of understanding and pity as she realised that he was creating a distraction, the ultimate distraction, so that she could escape.

Daunt and Drear were already fighting with each other to get to the blood flowing from his neck. The third one, who was back on his feet and fighting with Dread once more, turned and charged towards them, eager not to lose this unique opportunity, especially since Dread was unlikely to let him anywhere near the girl. That just left Dread, staring over at Fen, distracted enough to let Phoebe break away, and run off through the park. Dread hesitated, torn between chasing after the girl, and stopping to finish off Fen.

Phoebe glanced back and saw Fen lying on the ground, not moving, as three of the creatures flung themselves onto his body attempting to rip him apart, to swallow as much of the angel's blood as possible. He was submerged by his attackers, as the demons washed over him until he vanished from Phoebe's sight. It was like watching someone downing but being unable to help.

Saraf was looking up from the grass, finally registering what was happening to her friend, and Pam and Emily were so horrified that they stopped praying briefly and the light around them vanished.

Phoebe had no time to take in anymore. If she didn't escape, Fen's sacrifice was pointless, and she couldn't bear that.

'Don't let them drag you into the Darkness alive,' Fen had said to her. 'Better for you, and everyone else, to die here than there. And even if they cut you ... don't let them drink your blood.'

Phoebe glanced back. She had been standing on the lawn when Dread attacked her, now she was running across the grass. Any blood she'd shed so far might just have got soaked into the earth. She ripped some material from her skirt and wrapped it around her arm, tying to stop the blood from falling onto any hard surface where it might form a puddle. Then she ran, and kept running, until she was out of the park. A narrow road to her left sloped down towards the river and she fled down it, expecting Dread to catch up with her at any moment. An hour ago she would have said that she couldn't have run ten yards. Now she was pounding down the slope, running for her life. Well, not exactly her life, but to prevent the demons from getting the blood that was gushing out of her and there was only one way she could think of to do that.

When Phoebe reached the bottom of the road, she was on the brightly lit waterfront but she didn't look left or right to summon help. Instead she whispered a prayer – possibly the first one she'd ever spoken. Then she charged across the open pavement area, and flung herself into the river.

42

Fen had seen Phoebe take the chance he'd given her and run off into the Darkness, and almost sobbed with relief. He felt the pain as the demons' claws lacerated him, trying to access as much of his blood as they could swallow, but he didn't care. He had done all he could to help Phoebe, and if this was the price, he was willing to pay it. Better to lose everything protecting someone you cared about, than not to care at all.

He didn't know if Dread had followed the girl, or was one of the creatures attacking him, and he was too weak from loss of blood to open his eyes and look. So Fen didn't see Dire pick that moment to attack, the moment when Dread was deciding whether to chase the girl, or finish off the angel first: both were so tempting. But Dread never got the chance to make that decision. Dire came at him out of nowhere, attacking Dread when he was least expecting it, determined to get his revenge.

At first Pam and Emily didn't notice the additional demon that had suddenly appeared. Their eyes were fixed on Fen, horrified by what was happening to him. They began to pray again, and moved towards him, hoping that the prayer light surrounding them once more might at least drive the demons away from his body but before they reached him Saraf had got to her feet and was charging over to protect her friend. The three demons were bloated from drinking Fen's blood, and the smaller angel was furious with them. She began to pummel them with her fists, which, to be honest, wouldn't normally have had much effect, but to her surprise, as her blows landed, the creatures seemed to deflate, becoming smaller and weaker than they had ever been before. The fight went out of them completely, and they just keeled over and died.

'Did I do that?' Saraf asked Fen, shocked. Fen didn't answer. He couldn't. He could just about hear her voice, though it sounded a long way away, and he could feel her hand taking his, trying to comfort him. He felt her attempt to give him a hug and wanted to tell her off.

'No hugging,' he would have said, if he could, but jokingly, because the hug was comforting. It was good to have a friend with him as he died. He'd never been much of a one for friends… Fen regretted that now. He could hear Pam and Emily praying nearby, that was a blessing too, and he dimly realised that his blood seemed to have had a destructive effect on the demons which made his dying worthwhile.

'Phoebe,' he tried to say. He wanted to ask Saraf to look after the girl for him but he wasn't sure the words came out, as Fen let go of his life and prepared to go home.

Then he was gone, unaware of anything in this world anymore.

Saraf slowly got to her feet, ignoring the battle between the two surviving demons, and tugged at one of the roses that were caught on her robe. Pulling it free she laid it on Fen's chest. Then she turned tear filled eyes towards Pam and Emily.

'What should I do now?' she asked, feeling lost. Feeling like she had lost someone … someone close to her … not just Fen … but someone else too: a boy she could no longer remember.

'I think we'd better go after Phoebe,' said Emily.

'That's what Fen would want,' added Pam.

After a final glance at Dire and Dread, battling it out behind them, Pam, Emily and Saraf went to search for Phoebe.

As the sisters ran through the park, in the direction that Phoebe had taken, Saraf took to the air to search for the girl, calling out to Emily and Pam that she thought Phoebe was down by the river. The angel was wondering why the girl's silvery soul-light looked blurry, then she realised that Phoebe wasn't by the river, she was in it.

Dimly, Saraf realised that the fact she could see Phoebe's soul-light meant that she was no longer under Fen's protection, or any other angel's, and she knew that Fen would want her to help. Saraf was feeling so distressed herself that the effort felt almost beyond her. She drifted down through the air, until she was hovering just above the river.

Phoebe was struggling in the water, between the bridge and the bandstand, trying to pull herself towards the river's edge, but she was too weak. Saraf reached down and grabbed the girl by her hair, dragging her towards the river front. The angel couldn't lift Phoebe out of the water, but she could stop her being washed downstream by the current, and keep her head out of the river, until Pam and Emily reached them.

The two ladies, assisted by Saraf, managed to haul the young woman out of the water, and Pam knelt beside her.

'Why were you trying to kill yourself?' Pam asked, distressed. 'Fen just died trying to save you.'

'I wasn't,' spluttered Phoebe, weakly. 'Arm was bleeding … thought it would dilute my blood … stop demons getting it. Fen said not to let them … ' but the girl passed out before she could finish her explanation.

Pam dug into Phoebe's bag, which she was still carrying, pulled out the girl's mobile phone and called for an ambulance.

Emily was cradling Phoebe's head on her lap, trying to make her comfortable. She glanced over to Saraf, in her bloodstained robe, who was perched on top of the bandstand, rocking backwards and forwards, looking desolate.

'What's wrong with her?' Emily whispered to Pam.

'I don't think she's coping,' Pam replied, quietly. 'Watching Fen die was too much for her, I suspect.'

'I can understand that,' said Emily, who hadn't found it easy herself, and she had only met the angels that evening. She placed her hand on Phoebe's forehead; the girl felt cold and clammy. 'Where's this ambulance?'

'It'll be here soon, I'm sure,' said Pam, 'And when it arrives, make sure to tell them we're Phoebe's aunts. If they don't think we're her family they won't tell us what's going on.'

A few minutes later it arrived, and Phoebe, still

unconscious, was carefully loaded into it. The paramedics kindly allowed both Pam and Emily to travel to the hospital with them, to be near their 'niece.' They looked round for Saraf before climbing into the vehicle, but there was no sign of her.

43

Dire was enjoying himself. The rage that had built up inside him was finally being released as he smashed his fists repeatedly into Dread's face. He was dimly aware that the other demons were finishing off one of the angels, and that the girl had run off, but he wasn't about to let himself be distracted at this point. Dread was the one who had attacked and blinded him, the one who had left him for dead, the one who was about to pay for everything Dire had suffered.

Dread, of course, had forgotten all about Dire, assuming he had died in the Mithraic Temple underneath St Clemente's Basilica. Demons don't suffer from guilt or worry about consequences, and he hadn't given his victim a second thought. Now he was being pounded by a creature who, by rights, shouldn't even be alive, let alone be in Chester. It took him a couple of minutes to get to grips with what was happening and who was attacking him, which was more than long enough to give Dire the upper hand.

Dire managed to wrestle Dread to the ground, holding him down as he slashed at his enemy's throat again and again, just as Dread had slashed at his. Using the claws on his feet he kicked and tore at Dread's stomach, until that too was ripped open. Dread struggled to inflict some injuries in return, but he had left it too late. By the time he'd begun to respond the damage was done. He only managed to bite his opponent's face, ripping away a large piece of Dire's cheek, before his strength began to ebb away.

Dread couldn't believe it: he was a powerful demon, feared and hated by his fellow creatures in the Darkness. He was unstoppable, invincible, and on the path to all the power that drinking angel blood would bring, and now he was …

A final blow snapped Dread's neck.

Dire checked that the demon had indeed died. He wasn't about to get careless, as Dread had been with him, and find that he had created a powerful enemy who would come and attack him in the future. He was much too clever for that.

Once he was certain that his revenge was complete, Dire looked around. The humans had run away, there was a dead angel on the ground, and three other dead and deflated demons. Dire was relieved that he hadn't been tempted to taste the angel's blood before attacking Dread. It looked as if demons couldn't drink pure angel blood and survive, however much power they might derive from drinking it in its diluted form, from a human descendant. He took a moment to drag all five bodies into the bushes beside the path, feeling that the less humans learned about any of this the better, especially while he was still nearby.

Dire made his way out of the park, and began to cast about for any trace of the girl. He could no longer sense her because the effect of the blood he'd tasted in Rome had worn off but he had seen that she was losing blood. All he had to do was follow the trail.

He found one drop on the road running down to the river, but although he licked it up, he still couldn't sense what direction Phoebe had travelled in. He needed a bigger sample of her blood, to be able to track her.

Luckily for him, he found one. At the edge of the river he found the piece of material that Phoebe had ripped off her skirt to bind her bleeding arm. It had fallen off as she launched herself into the water. Some of the blood was drying already, but there was still enough moisture in the cloth for Dire to be able to suck up a little of it. He searched around for any larger puddles of blood, but the cloth seemed to be the only accessible trace the girl had left behind. Still, it was enough: he could sense her again. Probably not for long, but she couldn't have gone far in that state.

He'd be able to find her... Her and the baby within her, and as he was the last demon standing, he wouldn't have to share her blood. Better yet, he'd be free to drag her into the Darkness and kill her there. He remembered the legend. If a demon could do that to a human with angel blood, every demon would be free to over-run the world. And he'd have made it happen. He'd become the most powerful of them all.

He set off along the riverfront, searching for a way up into the city, heading for the place where he could sense the girl was. His vision was still limited, which still slowed him down a little, but he was bound to catch up with her soon. He just needed to be patient for a little while longer.

Phoebe was not in a good way. She was in the accident and emergency department of the hospital. She'd been rushed straight through to the resuscitation unit as soon as the paramedics lifted her out of the ambulance, as she was critically ill.

The junior doctor on duty when she first arrived wasn't sure where to start, since she was heavily pregnant, had an infected arm, was waterlogged and had obviously lost a lot of blood. He opted to deal with the blood loss first and set her up for a transfusion, sending a nurse to fetch some blood. The girl had lost so much blood that he struggled to get a line into her, as her veins had contracted. He called another doctor, and a couple of nurses over to help.

Pam and Emily watched through the window, concerned, as the four members of staff worked on Phoebe, desperate to get a line in so that they could start the transfusion before any of her internal organs packed up. Failing to get access to a vein in her arms or ankles, they tried her neck, and the sisters breathed a sigh of relief as the team nodded to each other and stepped back when they succeeded and the first doctor hooked Phoebe up to a bag of blood.

As one of the nurses came out through the swing doors, they heard the doctor calling after her.

'Make that four more units. She's going to need a lot of blood to get her stabilised.' The nurse nodded before she headed down the corridor. Meanwhile the doctor began to set up another drip, this one filled with antibiotics to treat the infection in Phoebe's arm.

Pam and Emily suddenly felt exhausted and went over to sit down on the seats that lined the corridor.

'This has been an interesting evening,' Emily said, conversationally. 'Quite enlightening, Pam. Care to fill me in?'

Pam told her sister about how she and her vicar, James, had gradually become drawn into dealing with certain 'situations,' and how that had led to their involvement with Phoebe, and everything that had happened since.

'I'm so sorry,' Pam said, as she finished her tale. 'I really didn't mean to bring trouble to your door like that. We hadn't expected the creatures to follow her here.'

'Nonsense,' replied Emily, firmly. 'I wouldn't have missed it for the world. I never imagined I'd meet angels ... or demons. Although it did get rather messier than I'd expected.'

The sisters fell silent, and Pam thought about Fen, offering himself up to buy Phoebe some time. She was determined that his efforts shouldn't be wasted. If Phoebe didn't have a guardian angel protecting her any more, it was down to her now.

'What about Saraf?' Emily asked.

'I don't know,' answered Pam. 'She's not officially in charge of Phoebe, and I get the feeling she doesn't cope with loss very well. She may have gone.'

'I suppose angels have to deal with a lot of loss.' Emily speculated. 'Even if they can keep their people safe from danger; everyone dies in the end.'

'True,' Pam agreed. 'Although I didn't know that angels could die.'

At that point the doctor came out to explain to them about Phoebe's treatment.

'We'll need to keep her in for a few days,' he explained.

'What about her baby?' Pam asked. 'Will it be all right?'

'We hope so,' the young man answered. 'Obviously the infection and possibly the blood loss, will have affected the baby too, but the transfusions and antibiotics will be reaching him or her, and that should sort out any problems the baby has. How long is it until the child is due?'

'About three weeks,' the sisters replied in unison.

The doctor smiled. 'That's good. If your niece does give birth earlier than expected, after all this trauma, at least the baby won't be considered premature. Better if it stays inside it's mum for now though, while we stabilise her.'

'Can we see her?' Pam asked.

'She's unconscious, but if you can give me a phone number, I'll get one of the nurses to give you a call in the morning, when she wakes up.'

Emily opened her mouth to give her home phone number, but Pam cut in, giving the doctor the number of the mobile in Phoebe's bag.

'What did you do that for?' whispered Emily as they walked away.

'We can't go back to your house, can we?' Pam replied. 'We don't know how many of those creatures are still around. There were two of them fighting it out when we left the park. One or both of them could still be looking for Phoebe, and your house is the first place they'd start.'

'Botheration,' said Emily crossly. 'I hadn't thought of that. Oh well, we'd better find somewhere to sleep. There's a cheap hotel not far from here.'

'That'll do!' agreed Pam, and the two of them set off.

44

Dire was following Phoebe's scent and moving towards where he sensed her blood was. Though, admittedly, the trace of her was fairly weak. He put that down to how much blood the girl had lost when Dread ripped her arm open, and as Dire himself hadn't been able to suck very much of her blood from the cloth he'd found, he thought that would explain his difficulty. The strange thing was that his sense of her location seemed to be getting weaker by the minute.

It had taken much longer to fade away the first time he'd tasted her blood. He couldn't understand it. He crept past the cathedral trying to keep out of sight. There were bound to be other guardian angels around watching over the city, even if the one who had protected the girl was dead. The last thing he wanted was to get spotted by anyone who might know what he was and try to stop him. He'd just reached the arch that went under the old Roman wall, when he lost her completely. It was as if she'd just vanished off the face of the earth. Or died, which would be really annoying after all the trouble the demons had gone through to catch up with her.

Realising that it would soon be light, Dire climbed up the steps onto the Roman Wall and followed the raised walkway to the left until he reached a sandstone tower, built where the wall changed direction, to run parallel to the river. There was a door with a pointed arch set into the base of the tower, made of thick old wood studded with blackened nails. Dire forced it open, entered the tower, and pushed the door closed behind him. He didn't want anyone coming in to investigate the damage. He just needed somewhere to hide during the day and rest. His injured throat and eyes were still painful and he needed to think. He wasn't about to stop looking for the girl - not now. He just needed to come up with a plan.

Pam and Emily were allowed in to see Phoebe in the morning, as soon as she regained consciousness. It was outside normal visiting hours but the girl was in such a state and so obviously in need of her aunts' support, that the ward sister agreed to make an exception for them. Besides, Phoebe had been put in a side room, so it wasn't as if her visitors were going to disturb the other patients.

'Last night,' Phoebe was asking, 'Did Fen get killed? I thought I saw him ... but I had to get away. I feel terrible for leaving him, and all of you, while that was going on.'

'You had to run, Phoebe,' Pam tried to reassure her. 'It was what Fen wanted. There would have been no point in offering himself up like that if it didn't help you to get away.'

'But he did die?' questioned Phoebe.

'I'm afraid so,' Emily replied. 'The demons ... well, let's just say pure angel blood doesn't agree with them.'

'So they're all dead? I'm safe now?'

Pam and Emily exchanged worried glances.

'I'm afraid not, dear,' said Pam. 'We think there are either one or two of them still out there.'

Phoebe turned her head away and looked out of the window beside her bed.

'The last few weeks have been like a bad dream ... and it's never going to stop, is it?' The girl avoided their eyes, hoping they wouldn't see the tears in hers. 'I'm going to have to keep running ... and Fen will have died for nothing.'

'Not for nothing,' said Pam gently. 'You're still alive and so is your baby. We just have to keep it that way.'

'And we've had an idea about that,' added Emily. 'You see, you've had a massive blood transfusion. Five units, the doctor said, which means that at the moment, for the next few days, your blood ...well, it's not really yours is it? It's mostly made up of all the donated blood they've put into you.'

'It's rather as if you're five other people at the moment,' chipped in Pam.

'So we don't think the creatures can track you down,' Emily concluded. 'Not until your body replaces the donated blood with its own. As far as we can work out, you should be safe for several days.'

'What about the baby? Will that have the donated blood in it too?' asked Phoebe, trying to sit up, as an idea occurred to her.

'I suppose so,' said Pam, 'since it will be getting its blood supply from you, and yours isn't your own.'

'It will be getting the antibiotics too,' said the nurse who came to check that all the drips Phoebe was attached to were working properly. 'Just as well. You need to stay here until we've beaten the infection in your arm. Those wounds have all been cleaned and stitched, but you will have scars, I'm afraid.'

'Inside and out,' thought Phoebe to herself, as the nurse went to tend to another patient.

'What about Saraf?' Phoebe asked. 'Is she dead too?'

'She's gone,' Pam answered, 'She helped pull you out of the river, but we haven't seen her since. She didn't take Fen's death very well.'

'She just seemed to sort of tune out,' explained Emily.

'So, no guardian angel then?' said Phoebe, turning the idea round in her head. 'Good! I don't want anyone else risking their lives to help me … human or angel. Enough people have died.' Besides, she couldn't bear to get attached to anyone else, she thought to herself, and then lose them too.

When the nurse came back to chivvy the sisters away, they headed to Emily's house in a taxi to collect a few overnight things.

'I'm worried about that girl,' announced Emily as she opened her front door.

'So am I,' agreed Pam. 'She's been through far too much, in such a short space of time. But I don't see what we can do about it.'

'Perhaps we should talk to your vicar friend … James, is it? Maybe he'll be able to come up with a way to help her.'

Staying at the house only long enough to phone James, and collect whatever they and Phoebe might need for the next couple of days, they took another taxi back to the hotel.

They both agreed that it would be harder for a demon to notice and follow them in a taxi than if they were on foot. But they were also extremely tired and glad of an excuse not to waste their energy tramping across the city, when they didn't know what their next challenge might be.

When James put the phone down after his call from Pam, he was stunned. He couldn't believe Fen was dead, or even that angels could die. He was worried that Saraf had vanished, leaving Phoebe without any heavenly protection.

Usually it was Celeste who contacted him, when the angels needed their 'second line of defence,' but he didn't know if she even knew what had happened to Fen, or to Phoebe. Perhaps this time he needed to contact her. He got down on his knees and prayed.

45

Dire came out of the tower at dusk and hurried to the house where Phoebe had been staying. The place was empty. There was no sign of the girl or the other two ladies. He'd hoped that the older women would be there, at least, and be foolish enough to lead him to Phoebe, but they weren't as stupid as he would have liked. He turned and headed back into the city. He knew the girl was injured, so if she wasn't at the house the obvious place to look for her was at a hospital. All he had to do was find it and there were always lots of signs to tell people where hospitals were. He didn't need to be able to sense the girl's blood to find her there. It would be easy.

Phoebe was lying in her hospital bed, turning ideas over in her mind. At the moment she was too weak to walk, and still connected to the drips that were treating her infection. If she could get well and get out of hospital quickly enough, she'd have a window of a few days when the demons couldn't track her.

If she left Chester, then and never went back to any of the people or places she'd been connected to before surely, she'd be safe and so would her baby. It was a painful idea, turning her back on Pam, Emily, and James who'd all given her so much help. Even worse was knowing that she'd never be able to get in touch with Giovanni again but it was worth it to protect her child. It all depended on her ability to get out of hospital in time.

Dire found the hospital easily enough. He waited until the lights were turned down on the wards, and the patients were being told to go to sleep, whether they wanted too or not.

With visiting hours over and fewer staff in the building, it was easier for him to make his way along the corridors, ducking into stairwells and storerooms if he heard anyone coming towards him. This would have been so much easier if he was in human form, he thought, but there was nothing he could do about that.

Eventually, he found the side room where Phoebe was being cared for. That answered his first question: she wasn't dead. The reason he hadn't been able to track her quickly became apparent too. There was another bag of blood being drip fed into her system as the doctors still weren't happy with her blood levels.

Which meant, of course, that she wouldn't be much use to him just then. No point in grabbing her and drinking her blood right then but perhaps he could kidnap her and get her back to the Darkness somehow. Her blood would eventually recover, then he could kill her. He leaned forward to take a closer look at her. Could he detach her from all this equipment? He didn't want to kill her, not yet anyway. His hand reached out towards her swollen belly, his claws twitching as he wondered if her baby still contained angel blood. Perhaps he could rip it out of her and carry it back to the Darkness instead. The thought played in his head for a while. What if the baby didn't survive the extraction? Both mother and baby could die and he'd be left with nothing.

He accidently bumped into the drip stand that held the liquid antibiotics, and it rattled against the metal frame of the bed. Phoebe opened her eyes and saw the demon crouching above her, his clawed hand over her unborn baby. She began to scream, as loudly as she could, and reached for the call button she'd been given too. As nurses came running into the room, Dire leapt for the window and started to scramble out of it. The first nurse to arrive got a glimpse of the demon as he dropped down from the window onto the roof of one of the laboratory buildings, but she didn't have time to look out of the window and see where the intruder went. Phoebe had started screaming again. A different kind of screaming this time … the shocked cry of a woman whose waters had just broken.

James's prayers seemed to have been answered. His message had somehow reached Celeste, who came to see him. Admittedly she woke him up in the middle of the night, and he felt a little embarrassed chatting to her in his pyjamas, especially as they were a silly Superman pair his sister had given him for Christmas. He filled the angel in on what had happened in Chester and asked if she knew about Fen's death.

'I didn't know we could die,' she explained, looking rather shocked. 'I've never heard of it happening before. So is Saraf watching over Phoebe now?'

'She's vanished, apparently,' said James. 'Helped pull Phoebe out of the river and hasn't been seen since.'

'She does that,' Celeste said with quiet resignation. 'We all struggle with loss. Over a lifetime we lose so many people. If you're trying to protect a whole city or town full of human, you're bound to lose some. In Fen's case he lost most of the people in the town he was protecting during an earthquake. The guilt nearly destroyed him. He was given smaller groups to protect, instead, that's what the High Council does if angels aren't able to function at full strength anymore. If the stress is getting to them. He was just given individuals to look after that, but he couldn't connect to any of them.'

'He connected with Phoebe,' James pointed out. 'He must have done, to die for her.'

'True,' Celeste agreed, thoughtfully. 'I'm really glad he did. That was what he needed, even if it led to his own death. But Saraf … she's never coped with loss at all. When she loses someone, even if she's looked after them all their life, and they die naturally of old age … she can't handle it. She just sort of … blanks them. It's as if they never existed. If she doesn't have a tangible memento of them, she forgets them completely.'

'That's tragic,' James said, feeling sad for the childlike angel.

'It protects her from the pain,' said Celeste, having a little understanding of how Saraf sometimes felt.

For the first time James noticed that Celeste had a few faint lines of sorrow around her dark green eyes, and that her long red hair was a little lighter than when he had first met her. He'd been so dazzled by meeting an angel, at the time, that he hadn't paid as much attention as he would have done on meeting another human. He only saw her when there was a crisis to deal with, which didn't leave a lot of time for such observations. Now he could see a little of the strain she was under, although he knew she'd never complain about it.

'But Saraf loses the happy memories too,' James said. 'The friendships, the connections she's made. The sense of having done everything she could for the person she protected.'

'That's Saraf,' Celeste nodded sadly. 'She'll reappear in a while complaining that she hasn't been assigned to anyone for hundreds of years, and why don't we put her to work? And we will … until the next time grief gets to her, and she disappears again.'

'So she's not going to turn up to protect Phoebe or the baby?' James concluded.

'No, she can't. She can never go back to people she's known in her past.' Celeste looked sad for a moment, then pulled herself together. 'The High Council have assigned me to protect Phoebe, which makes sense now I know that Fen is dead.'

'But won't that leave the High Council, and those of you that deal with incursions, shorthanded?' James asked.

'Yes,' sighed Celeste. 'But what else can we do? Too few angels, too many people. That's why so few humans have their own individual guardian angel. We barely have the manpower to protect everyone, even when you're all clumped together in cities.' She smiled at him, adding, 'You may find you get called on more often, I'm afraid.'

'I can handle it. But what about Phoebe? She says she doesn't want protecting. She refuses to have another guardian angel,' James said. 'Pam thinks Phoebe can't cope with the idea of anyone else dying either.'

'Don't worry,' said Celeste with a gentle smile. 'I'll make sure she never knows I'm there.'

46

When Pam and Emily arrived at the hospital to visit Phoebe the next day, they were greeted by the sight of her cradling a little baby girl in her arms. Pam wondered why the hospital hadn't phoned to tell them, then realised that Phoebe's mobile needed charging. They plugged it in next to her bed, leaving the phone within reach on her bedside unit, and spent the next few minutes making a fuss of both Phoebe and the baby.

'Is she healthy?' Pam asked, 'Can they tell yet if the infection did her any harm?'

'They're treating her with antibiotics, just in case,' Phoebe explained, 'But they think she's fine,' the girl smiled, 'And I think she's perfect. She's got Marco's eyes.'

'What are you going to call her?' asked Emily.

'I'm not,' replied Phoebe. Seeing their puzzled glances, she quickly added, 'Not yet, anyway. I want to get to know her a little first. Would you do me a favour? My camera is in my shoulder bag. I can't reach it from here.'

Pam hunted through the bag and found Phoebe's camera, and they spent a happy few minutes taking photographs of each of them holding the baby. When the camera stopped working Emily gave it back to Phoebe.

'The roll of film is all used up, I'm afraid,' said Emily. 'You need one of those new digital cameras. You can take a lot more photos with those.'

'Would you be able to get them printed up for me?' Phoebe asked. 'As quickly as possible? There are pictures of Marco on there, I think. I really want to show this little one what he looked like.' There was an urgency to her request that Pam found worrying, but she was happy to agree to do as the girl asked. Anything to give her young friend some peace of mind.

'We can do it as soon as we leave,' said Emily cheerfully.

'There's a camera shop nearby. I think they process films in an hour or two.'

'What's the rush?' Pam asked. 'You're safe here for a few days, aren't you? The demons can't track you at the moment?'

'They can't track me, but they can find me,' she answered. 'There was one here last night. That's what sent me into labour. I suppose it's logical. You don't have to be able to track my blood to know that I'm so badly injured I'd need to be in hospital.'

'So you and the baby need to leave as soon as possible,' stated Pam.

'As soon as I'm strong enough, and we've both finished the antibiotics we're on.'

'Right,' said Emily decisively, 'We'd better get the tyres sorted on both our cars, Pam, in case we need to be ready to make a quick getaway. We can go back to my house now we know that the demon doesn't need to follow us to find you. I'll show you where the camera shop is, and you can get the photos printed while I sort out the cars.'

They said goodbye to Phoebe and the baby and hurried off to do their errands.

Phoebe didn't have the heart to tell them that they wouldn't be driving her and the baby anywhere. That nowhere would be safe for her child if the two of them were together.

Dire was back in his hiding place in the tower. He realised that there was no point in grabbing the girl, or her baby, just yet but he could wait. They would recover soon enough, and come out of the hospital. He might not be able to track the girl, but he could recognise her and snatch her away. Or at least snatch the baby, once it was born. After all this trouble, he wasn't about to go back to the Darkness empty handed.

Phoebe was drowsing in bed, the baby sleeping beside her, when her mobile rang.

It was Giovanni, calling her from Rome, to see how she was

doing. Phoebe poured out everything that had happened, her injury, her grief at Fen's death, her decision about the baby, thankful to have someone she could talk to. She knew that if she told Pam and Emily what her plans were, they'd try to make her change her mind.

Of course, Giovanni wanted to stop her too, but he was in Rome and was too far away to be able to intervene, so she could be honest with him. Honesty turned out to be a bad idea. Giovanni was livid - not that it was anything to do with him - and the argument that followed reduced Phoebe to tears. Even so, she wouldn't change her mind. This was for the best, as hard as it was going to be.

That evening not only Pam and Phoebe came to visit her, but James arrived as well. Pam had told him that Phoebe had had the baby, and he jumped straight in his car and drove to Chester. Phoebe was delighted to see him again, and even more so when she heard what he suggested.

'A baptism? Here in the hospital?' Phoebe said wonderingly.

'Yes,' said James, 'But Pam tells me you don't have a name for the baby yet. So perhaps just a blessing service? Let's claim her for the good guys eh? Give her all the protection we can.'

'Yes,' said Phoebe, smiling. 'That would be perfect.'

It was a simple service, just four adults and the baby in the hospital room, with Celeste, unacknowledged and invisible, outside the door. Pam had not only had Phoebe's photos printed, she'd put a new roll of film in her camera.

Phoebe made sure she took pictures with all of them, her wonderful 'second line of defence,' knowing she might not see any of them again for a long time, if ever. James, in particular, looked very soppy as he held the baby, and Phoebe wanted to capture that moment to remember it. Eventually the nurse came in to send the visitors away.

'When you're out of hospital,' said James as he left, 'I'll go to The Hell-Fire Caves and open up the that weak spot. If the demon can't find you, he's likely to head back there. Once he's gone through, I'll seal it up again, and you and the baby will be safe. Now sleep tight, and God Bless.'

Phoebe lay there after they'd gone, wishing she could have told them her plan, said goodbye properly and explained that she didn't think she and the baby would ever be truly safe, even if the demon was locked back into the Darkness. It had come through once; it could come through again and it knew all about her.

The hospital had told her she was being discharged in the morning: she didn't have long. She opened the packet of photographs that Pam had brought her. There were some pictures of her and Marco on their graduation day, only a few weeks ago. Images of The Hell-Fire Caves, including the one of Marco in front of the Inner Temple. It was such a good picture of him, but knowing what she now knew, the setting freaked her out. And there were the photos of Nonna Battista, some of Giovanni, and of Fen and Saraf. Phoebe was amazed those had come out. The pictures of the demons were there too, along with the baby photos they'd taken that morning. Shoving the demon pictures to the bottom of the pile, Phoebe started to hold up each image in front of her new-born child.

'This is your daddy. He would have loved you very much. And here is your great-grandmother - your Nonna. That's Italian for granny ... Nonna Battista. Here's Giovanni, your daddy's best friend. These are all part of your family. So are these,' Phoebe added, holding up the photos of Fen and Saraf.

Of course, Phoebe knew that her daughter wouldn't be able to focus on the images, or understand the words, but she wanted the child to feel part of a family, to feel loved, and she couldn't think of any other way to do it ... not when she had so little time.

Outside the door, Celeste was feeling concerned. Phoebe definitely had a plan but what was it?

47

Phoebe had packed her bags as soon as it was light. Pam and Emily had brought all of her luggage from the house a couple of days ago, because they didn't know what she'd want. She'd found moving around her hospital room harder than she had expected. Her limbs were swollen and she was covered in bruises, both from the demon attack, and the medical teams' attempts to get a line into her veins. How on earth was she going to manage?

She slumped down on the bed and hugged Marco's jumper, but even that couldn't give her much comfort. The smell of him was beginning to fade. Phoebe had never felt so alone. She looked at her precious photos again. There were some lovely ones of the baby, from the day before. She decided she might as well use up the roll of film in the camera, and take as many pictures of the baby as she could. She knew this would be her last chance.

She'd almost finished when Giovanni burst in through the door. How he'd managed to find her, at dawn, without being stopped by the hospital staff, she had no idea, but she wished he hadn't.

'You cannot do this,' he announced, before he had even crossed the room.

'Good morning to you too!' snapped Phoebe. 'And I can. She's my baby and I have to do what's best for her.'

'How can this be what is best?' he argued.

'You don't have the right to tell me what to do to protect my own child. And don't shout, you'll wake her up.'

Giovanni moved softly over to the cot, where the baby was sleeping.

'Hello little one,' he said, gazing down on her in wonder. 'She is so beautiful. Marco's little girl.'

'And mine,' said Phoebe. 'Marco isn't here ... I'm the one who has to decide what's best for her now … and I have.'

'Are you sure you can't just bring her to Rome?' he asked, calmer now. 'I'll help you to protect her.'

'They followed us to Rome once before. She's no safer there than here.'

Reluctantly, Giovanni nodded, 'But this seems so hard, on you, and on her.' He crossed the room and put his arm around her shoulders. 'Too hard to do on your own.'

'You'll come with me?' She asked, surprised. Giovanni nodded.

'On one condition,' he added. 'Let me hold the little one, even if it is just this once.'

Phoebe smiled, and gently lifted the sleeping child into his arms. She looked so comfortable there, that Phoebe wanted to weep. Instead, she picked up the camera and took a photo of him cradling his best friend's baby. Putting the camera back in her shoulder bag, she glanced round the room to make sure she hadn't forgotten anything. Then she nodded to Giovanni.

'It's time,' she said.

They walked in silence through the streets in the early morning light, Giovanni carrying Phoebe's small amount of luggage, while she carried the sleeping baby. She had to admit, to herself at least, that she couldn't have managed without his help, she was still so weak. When they were nearing the cathedral Giovanni finally spoke.

'Which door? It is a big building, yes? It will have more than one door.'

Phoebe thought about the activity she'd seen there earlier in the week. The great front doors opened onto the street, but the back ones were reached by a few steps leading down from the Abbey Green. They were more sheltered, and more likely to be used by the cathedral staff. By people who might want to do what was right by the child. And they would arrive early in the morning, from the list of service times she'd seen.

'The back door,' she answered, turning under the great

sandstone arch that led to the Abbey Green. She walked around the green, towards the rear of the cathedral and down the steps. Phoebe wrapped the baby in several pieces of her own clothing, making sure they had no labels that might lead back to her. Then she and Giovanni knelt in front the doors, said a prayer for the child - led by Giovanni, since Phoebe didn't have any idea how to start.

They stood up, collected Phoebe's bags, and walked away from the cathedral.

Celeste looked on, horrified. This was Phoebe's plan? To abandon the baby?

She followed the two of them as they went under the arch, and reached the street, wondering whether she should appear to Phoebe, tell her to change her mind. Then she saw a creature. A demon she vaguely recognised from the fight in Stow, lurking in a doorway.

The creature glanced at the young couple, and looked away. He looked back again and shook his head. His eyes were still scarred and blurry.

Dire was keeping those damaged eyes peeled for a pregnant woman, or one with a baby. Running and hiding. Not a young couple out for an early morning stroll. And yet the two of them looked familiar. Perhaps he should follow them? Before he had a chance to move, an angel landed in front of him and he found himself in a fight. Celeste was brutal. Taking in the creature's injuries, she aimed for his eyes and throat inflicting so much damage that the demon eventually broke away, and ran for cover, racing along the road, up onto the city walls and back to his tower. He'd had enough. He needed to get back to the Darkness, where he could recover … Gain power, and wait for an opportunity to go after the girl and her baby again.

Celeste looked round when the demon had fled. There was no sign of Phoebe or her friend, and when she hurried back to where the baby had been left, she saw a couple of members of the cathedral staff crouched beside it. One of them was already using a mobile to call for assistance. It looked like Phoebe's decision was final, and Celeste could understand why the young mother had made it. If the baby had no connection to its mother whatsoever, it could grow up in safety. Even if the demons tracked Phoebe down, they'd never find her child, or know where to find the little girl who had angel blood running through her veins.

Pam was up and about early that morning. She needed to be ready to go if Phoebe was well enough to leave the hospital; although she didn't know where to take the young woman. Would anywhere be safe for her and her baby? Pam also had some unfinished business to attend to. She wanted to return to the scene of the final battle between Fen and the demons. She had seen Saraf searching for something there. Something that seemed to matter desperately to the young angel. Pam wanted to find it.

Of course, several days had passed since then, and Pam had no real expectation of finding anything. People walked though Grosvenor Park all the time, anybody could have found whatever it was, still, it was worth a try.

When she reached the battleground it seemed strangely peaceful, considering what had happened there just a few nights ago. Pam knelt on the grass, where she'd seen Saraf searching. She knew she looked ridiculous, but wasn't going to let that bother her, as she felt around with her fingers, trying to find anything that the angel might have considered precious.

She had searched for twenty minutes, and was ready to give up, when she felt something sharp against her fingers. Tugging it out of the ground, where it must have been pressed by demon feet during the struggle, she found it was a cross, very old and intricate, and probably made of silver, from the look of it.

Pam didn't know its significance to Saraf, but she was glad she'd managed to find it for her, even if she wasn't sure how to return it. She'd keep it safe for the little angel until she had the opportunity to do so. As she got back to her feet, she noticed a couple of large white feathers, bent and twisted, lying at the base of a bush near the edge of the path. Feeling almost certain that the feathers had belonged to Fen, she picked those up too, and tucked them into her bag along with the cross.

When she returned to Emily's house, she found her sister looking grief-stricken.

'It was on the radio,' Emily explained. 'A baby has been found abandoned at the cathedral. It must be Phoebe's. I rang the hospital and they said she'd discharged herself early this morning.'

'If it is Phoebe's baby,' announced Pam staunchly, 'Then she hadn't been abandoned. She's been entrusted to the cathedral, and to God, to keep her safe!'

Pam shook her head, a sad smile on her face that matched Emily's. They were struggling to come to terms with Phoebe's decision, but beginning to understand it too. This was Phoebe's way of protecting her child, and saving her from a lifetime of being on the run from demons who wanted her blood.

Just then they heard a sniggering sound coming from the cupboard under the stairs. Emily picked up her handbag and marched towards cupboard, flinging the door open. She discovered two ugly little creatures cowering inside.

'What are those?' she asked Pam.

'Imps,' her sister replied. 'They are probably the consequence of you finding out more than you're supposed to. There are always consequences. Still, these ones seem harmless enough - as infestations of imps go. A bit pathetic really. But then, we didn't break the rules in a major way by telling you what was going on. You couldn't help but see the angels and the demons.'

'Harmless? They've poured all my cleaning liquids onto the floor, shredded my dusters, and smeared shoe polish on the inside of the door! How do we get rid them?'

'I'll go and get the Holy Water,' said Pam, but before she could turn away, the imps made a break for it, leaping out through the cupboard door. Emily swung her handbag, and knocked first one to the floor, then the other. Pam prodded their inert bodies and discovered that both the imps were unconscious. After a moment the creatures just fizzled away back into the Darkness.

'Whatever do you keep in your handbag, Emily?' asked Pam, impressed.

'Half a brick,' replied Emily, smugly, 'I put it in there the night of the demon attack. I thought it might make a useful weapon.'

'It seems you were correct.' Pam said 'Put the kettle on, will you? I really need a cup of tea.'

'We both do,' added Emily, with a grin.

48

Dire hid in his tower until dusk, the freshly reopened wounds on his eyes and neck seeping dark, corrupted ichor which oozed down his face and chest, sticking to him and making him even more uncomfortable. Even the spikes on his head ached.

He'd had enough, for now, anyway. He needed to get back to the Darkness, and the only place he could start was the place where he had come through into the world. As soon as it was dark enough, he went looking for a lorry heading south. It took him four trucks and most of the night, but eventually he found himself near The Hell-Fire Caves and walked the last couple of miles to get to them.

It was only seven o'clock in the morning, and he was surprised to find the recently repaired gates were already open. He entered the stone tunnels hesitantly, suspecting a trap of some kind, but nothing leapt out to attack him as he made his way to the furthest point … the Inner Temple.

The cross set into the floor, and the other protections that had sealed the route through to the Darkness had been removed. Somebody had prepared a way home for him. He looked around, wondering if the somebody was still there.

Sure enough, he could see a man tucked behind one of the stalagmites in the River Styx section of the caves. He was trying to stay out of sight. Much as Dire wanted to get back to the Darkness, he didn't want some human's help to do it, and he didn't want to go back empty handed, either. The demon splashed into the water and pulled the figure out onto the passageway in front of the Inner Temple.

James had been taken by surprise, and the demon thought the human would be easy to overpower. Dire could see the man's orangey yellow soul-light flickering inside him, already turning icy-blue with fear, and the demon was determined to collect it and take it back into the Darkness with him. At least then his time in the world wouldn't have been completely wasted. Not that demons had the right to collect the soul-light of any human who didn't make the mistake of inviting them into the world, but he was well past caring about that. Demons really weren't that bothered about rules.

James struggled as the demon grabbed his throat, feeling overwhelmed with panic. Then he remembered to start praying. Soon a pale light encircled him, making the demon's hands, that were in contact with his throat, burning hot. Dire was tempted to snatch his hands away, but he was even more tempted to hold on tight, choke the man, and swallow his soul-light as it escaped from the dying body.

Lack of oxygen was making James light-headed, and he could barely think. He stopped praying and the demon grunted in satisfaction, as the prayer light faded and the burning sensation in the creature's clawed hands faded with it. James was angry at himself for coming to the caves alone, for thinking he didn't need help. He'd been so wrong, and now he thought he was about to pay for that mistake with his life.

Suddenly the demon released him, dropping James's body to the ground. Twisting his head to find out who had come to his rescue, he was surprised to see Saraf beating the creature with a large metal cross, driving it towards the weak spot in the Inner Temple. The usually calm, cheerful angel seemed to be taking a considerable amount of rage out on the demon in front of her, and the creature couldn't help but back away from her attack.

When it reached the point where the Darkness seemed to be in contact with the world, the demon vanished, back to where it had come from.

James scrambled to his feet and hurried forward to begin the process of sealing the way between the Darkness and the world with prayers and Holy Water. He realised that the cross Saraf had used to attack the demon was the one that he'd dug up from the floor, to open the route up again. He gently removed it from her fingers and cemented it back in position. Only when the weak spot was well and truly sealed did he sink to the floor, to catch his breath.

'Thank you,' he said to Saraf, his voice hoarse.

'You're welcome,' she said, primly.

'I didn't expect to see you again,' James remarked, smiling at her. She gave him a puzzled look.

'Do you know me?' she asked. James's heart sank. She didn't remember him, so she probably didn't remember anything else about the last few weeks either.

'Why are you here?' James questioned gently, not wanting to unsettle her. 'If you don't remember me, then you didn't come to help ... not on purpose. So why did you come here?'

'I don't know,' she answered. 'I can't remember. I was searching for ... I don't know ... something ... someone. And I just remembered this place, so I came.'

'Well, I'm very glad you did,' said James gratefully. 'My name's James, by the way, and you just saved my life but then, that's what you do, isn't it?'

'Is it?' Saraf looked surprised. 'If you say so.'

She turned and began to walk away. She paused, looking back over her shoulder at him, a confused expression on her face. 'Nice to meet you, James,' she said, then she skipped slowly up the corridor and out of sight.

James took a moment to say a prayer for the poor, lost creature. Then he cleared up any signs of his confrontation with the demon, and made one more check that the weak spot was properly sealed, before leaving the caves and going home.

Phoebe was sitting beside Giovanni on the plane to Rome. They were both very quiet, and tears were rolling down Phoebe's face, though she tried not to sob out loud. Some of her tears fell onto her bandaged arm. She supposed she'd have to get the dressings changed at some point, and get the stitches taken out but it was all too much to think about at the moment.

'What will you do now?' Giovanni asked, more to break the silence than because he expected her to have a plan. Phoebe shrugged... She couldn't think about anything except the child she'd left behind.

'I can't go to Nonna Battista's house,' was all she could think of to say.

'Then you must come to mine,' he said, 'For tonight, anyway. It's just a flat, not a house, but I can sleep on the sofa. You can have my room. You know that they can't find you. Not yet. Stay at mine. Come to Nonna Battista's funeral tomorrow, you wanted to do that anyway. Then we'll work out what to do.' She nodded, too tired to argue.

She no longer had the strength to run, or to fight. She was content to let Marco's best friend, who was now her friend, help her, for a little while at least, until she was ready to make her own decisions again. There would never be another decision as difficult as the one she had just made. The one that involved giving up her daughter forever, to keep the child safe.

Back in the Darkness, Dire was prowling around. He was angry and he took his fury out on any passing imps and shouted at other demons. He saw Glint, the imp that had found the weak spot between the worlds and kept the information to himself. Grasping the smaller creature by the neck, he flung the imp into a cage and ordered some of the other imps to torture him again. He might as well take his pleasures where he could find them. He noticed one of the imps was trying to slide away, ignoring his command. He lifted that one up too, by its scrawny little arm, and shook it.

'You were Dread's imp, weren't you?' Dire asked. 'Snot? Slug? Snig! That was it!' Snig squirmed in the demon's claws. 'Well you're my imp now, and if I give you an order, you obey it. Torture that imp!'

He dropped Snig to the floor, and the imp shrugged apologetically at Glint, before reluctantly joining the rest of his fellows in torturing the imp he had helped to rescue. What choice did he have?

Dire couldn't believe his misfortune. He had come so close to getting hold of a human with angel blood. That would have made him incredibly powerful, and yet he'd failed, which left him feeling humiliated.

Still, every so often the rules got broken, foolish humans invited demons into the world thinking, wrongly, that they could control the creatures of the Darkness and when that happened, he'd be ready. He wouldn't let that girl escape a second time. He knew who she was and what she looked like. One way or another, he was going to get hold of her, and her baby. All he had to do wait!

ABOUT THE AUTHOR

Fiona Angwin was born and brought up on the Wirral Peninsula and has been addicted to books, animals and theatre since she was a child. This has led to a rather varied career. She did a Zoology degree at Liverpool University, followed by drama training, and has juggled acting, writing, directing, theatre administration, being a bat worker and environmental educationalist, and working as a zookeeper/presenter at Chester Zoo for a couple of years. As well novels, she Fiona has written a number of plays and musicals for the theatre companies she's worked with.

Now living in South Wales, Fiona works as The Yarn Spinner - a storyteller and puppeteer. This involves building many of the unique puppets.

For more information visit www.fionaangwin.com

Other Published Works

SOUL-LIGHTS
SOUL-SCARS
MANX TALES

Other Telos Titles

DAVID J HOWE
TALESPINNING

FREDA WARRINGTON
NIGHTS OF BLOOD WINE

PAUL LEWIS
SMALL GHOSTS

DAWN G HARRIS
DIVINER

STEVE LOCKLEY & PAUL LEWIS
KING OF ALL THE DEAD

SIMON MORDEN
ANOTHER WAR

GRAHAM MASTERTON
THE HELL CANDIDATE
THE DJINN
RULES OF DUEL (WITH WILLIAM S BURROUGHS)
THE WELLS OF HELL

RAVEN DANE
ABSINTHE AND ARSENIC
DEATH'S DARK WINGS

CYRUS DARIAN STEAMPUNK SERIES
CYRUS DARIAN AND THE TECHNOMICRON
CYRUS DARIAN AND THE GHASTLY HORDE
CYRUS DARIAN AND THE WICKED WRAITH

SAM STONE

THE VAMPIRE GENE SERIES

Horror, thriller, time-travel series.

1: KILLING KISS

2: FUTILE FLAME

3: DEMON DANCE

4: HATEFUL HEART

5: SILENT SAND

6: JADED JEWEL

JINX CHRONICLES

Hi-tech science fiction fantasy series

1: JINX TOWN

2: JINX MAGIC

3: JINX BOUND

KAT LIGHTFOOT MYSTERIES

Steampunk, horror, adventure series

1: ZOMBIES AT TIFFANY'S

2: KAT ON A HOT TIN AIRSHIP

3: WHAT'S DEAD PUSSYKAT

4: KAT OF GREEN TENTACLES

5: KAT AND THE PENDULUM

6: TEN LITTLE DEMONS

THE COMPLETE LIGHTFOOT

THE DARKNESS WITHIN

Science Fiction Horror Short Novel

CTHULHU AND OTHER MONSTERS

ZOMBIES IN NEW YORK AND OTHER BLOODY JOTTINGS

Short story collections

BRYONY PEARCE

WAVEFUNCTION

WINDRUNNER'S DAUGHTER

TANITH LEE
TANITH LEE A TO Z
BLOOD 20
DEATH OF THE DAY

STEPHEN LAWS
SPECTRE

SIMON CLARK
THE FALL
HUMPTY'S BONES

HELEN MCCABE
THE PIPER TRILOGY
1: PIPER
2: THE PIERCING
3: THE CODEX

PAUL FINCH
CAPE WRATH & THE HELLION
TERROR TALES OF CORNWALL (Editor)
TERROR TALES OF NORTH WEST ENGLAND (Editor)

SOLOMON STRANGE
THE HAUNTING OF GOSPALL

BRAM STOKER
DRACULA

DACRE STOKER
STOKER ON STOKER

TELOS PUBLISHING
www.telos.co.uk